THE SKETCHER

LEEIA L. HENDERSON

Copyright © 2022 by Leeia L. Henderson

All rights reserved. This book or any portion thereof may not be reproduced or transmitted in any form or manner, electronic or mechanical, including photocopying, recording, or by any information storage or retrieval system, without the express written permission of the copyright owner except for the use of brief quotations in a book review or other noncommercial uses permitted by copyright law.

Printed in the United States of America

ISBN: Softcover   979-8-88622-180-0
       eBook   979-8-88622-181-7
Republished by: PageTurner Press and Media LLC
Publication Date: 04/05/2022

To order copies of this book, contact:
PageTurner Press and Media
Phone: 1-888-447-9651
info@pageturner.us
www.pageturner.us

THE SKETCHER

It was a cold rainy Monday morning here in Seattle. I was in bed sound asleep, tired from giving a going away party for three homeless teenagers who lived with us for five years. Then my alarm clock went off; I looked over and it was 7:00 a.m. I really didn't want to get up, but I had to eat breakfast.

After getting dressed, I headed down the hall to the girls' section where my daughter slept. When I walked in, all the girls were gone except for my thirteen-year old daughter Honesty. She was sitting on the side of her bed staring at the wall.

I asked her, "Why aren't you dressed for breakfast?" She responded not.

I walked over to her closet to find her something to wear. I ask Honesty if she has an outfit she liked most, but she just kept staring. All of a sudden, my daughter frantically started to shake, as if she was having a seizure. She fell to the floor rolling back and forth kicking violently. I ran over to hold her down; and as I was holding her arms, she let out a scream, and when she opened her eyes the white part had turned all black, then shifted back to normal, then they started to bleed. I let go of her and jumped back because it scared me. At this point, I yelled for help. Next thing I knew my daughter had passed out.

All this took place in a shelter we lived in. Due to my back surgery, I wasn't able to return to work, so I lost my job and the home I and her father was buying. As for Honesty's father Jeremiah, he walked out of our life when she was one year old, for a good paying job in Sacramento, California, but we never heard from him since he got that job. We have been homeless now for six months, but some good has happened since I have been here at the shelter. I became a Christian. As for my daughter Honesty, she has an incredible gift that I'm so grateful for. She is a sketch artist and people pay her to sketch them, and this is how we are able to get food and clothes to add to what the shelter provides.

Meanwhile, as my daughter was having this terrifying experience, two of the staff members ran into the room responding to the loud scream they heard.

Staff member one: We heard a scream. What happened?

Journey: It was Honesty. When I walked in her room this morning, she was sitting on the side of her bed staring at the wall. I went to look for something for her to wear when all of a sudden she started shaking and kicking violently and rolling around on the floor. Then the white of her eyes turned black, then back to normal. They changed a few more times, then they started to bleed, and that is when she let out that horrifying scream.

Staff member two: Well, her eyes are not bleeding now. And where is the blood? I think she needs to go to the hospital. I will call an ambulance to take you both there and we will pay for it.

Journey: But they were bleeding! I do not understand . . . wait! Before we go, I remember when we first came here that the policy was that if someone left for any reason and wasn't back by a certain time, they would lose their sleeping space.

Staff member one: Yes, this is true, only if that person is gone overnight. After that, if someone comes in who really needs a bed then we have to give that spot to that person.

Journey: I understand.

Staff member two: Journey! The ambulance is here.

When the ambulance arrived, they took Honesty's vital signs; and as they were taking them, she started to shake again then she stopped. They put her in the ambulance and I climbed in the back with her. While I was sitting there I held her hand, I was telling her that she was going to be all right and not to worry, but she just lie there with her eyes closed.

After a twenty-minute ride, we arrived at the hospital. They wasted no time getting Honesty into the ER. Once we were inside, the nurse must have spoken to the shelter because they took my daughter straight to the examination room. Next thing I knew, the doctor walked in.

Dr. Smith: Hello, I'm Dr. Smith, and this must be Honesty. Tell me what is going on with your daughter.

Journey: I do not know. All I know is this morning I went into her room, and when I opened the door, she had this blank look on her face and was staring at the wall. She then started shaking and rolling around on the floor. Then I ran over to hold her down. While I was holding her down, she let out a terrifying scream. I looked at her and when I did, the white of her eyes was all black, then they shifted back to normal, then they started to bleed.

Dr. Smith: They started to bleed? Let me look at her eyes

When the doctor went to touch Honesty's eyes, she swiftly grabbed his wrist, but her eyes remained closed. I jumped and Dr. Smith pulled his wrist away.

Journey: Why did she do that?

Dr. Smith: Wow! She has much strength. I would say reflex, but not for sure. Tell me how old is Honesty?

Journey: She's thirteen.

Dr. Smith had a puzzled look on his face.

Dr. Smith: Hmmm. You said both eyes went all black and no white showing, then they went back to normal, then they started to bleed. Hmmm. With her eyes being closed, I cannot see them. I am going to have to keep her overnight to run some tests.

Journey: Oh no! She cannot stay overnight. You see, Doctor, we live in a shelter, and if we are gone more than a day, we will lose our beds.

Dr. Smith: Is it Mrs. or Miss?

Journey: Miss Brown.

Dr. Smith: Miss Brown, I am sorry about having to keep your

daughter overnight, but I have no choice. It is our procedure.

So they rolled Honesty down for tests. I knew after all this was over, I would have to look for us a place to stay. We would be on the streets living until then. While I was sitting in the waiting room, a woman in her late forties, about 5'9, with long brown hair and eyes, dressed well, smelled good, came up to me and said with a slight New York accent.

Lady with New York accent: Excuse me, how are you? I couldn't help overhearing your conversation with Dr Smith. I was in the next room and I heard you telling him you and your daughter are living ina shelter and if you're not back within a certain time, that you would lose your spot. Oh, sorry, I'm Jania Humphrey.

Journey: Hi, nice to meet you. People call me Miss Brown, but my name is Journey, and yes, it is true my daughter and I will have to look for a place to live.

Jania: Well, my husband and I just moved here to Seattle from New York to continue our business in real estate. In addition, we just bought a home. I know this may sound a little strange considering you don't know me, but would you like to stay with us until your daughter gets better?

Journey: I-I I'm not sure, but they're keeping her overnight.

Jania: No problem, I will give you my cell number, and when all is said and done call me.

Journey: Oh, okay, thank you.

After she left, I thanked God for sending her my way. She seemed nice and I felt comfortable for some reason. By this time, I was starting to feel tired. I looked at my watch, two hours had passed, and Honesty was still being tested. I thought I would get some shut-eye. As soon as I closed my eyes, this nurse tapped me on my shoulder and said the doctor wanted to see me. When I walked into the room, there was my daughter lying asleep hooked up to monitors and IV.

Dr. Smith: Let us step out for a sec. We ran all types of tests, and to our surprise we found out that Honesty has become blind. This is very strange and unusual for this to happen to someone her age. However, you should find her a doctor to further check her condition out.

Journey: Oh no! She is blind! How can this be? She was fine last night!

Dr. Smith: Miss Brown, calm down. We do not know how this happened to your daughter. It is very unusual for someone to become blind overnight. However, I am sure there are some cases out there; we just have to do some research.

Journey: There is something you don't know. Honesty is a great sketch artist and she does this for a living. And in order for her to sketch, as you know, she have to be able to see.

Dr. Smith: Well, there are schools for the blind, but we will talk about that later. For now, we are going to put Honesty in a room where you and her can rest, this way we can keep an eye on her just for tonight.

After talking to the doctor, I returned to the examining room. Honesty was still resting. Later a nurse came in to transport us to a better room. When we got to the room, it was so nice that I wanted to live there; it had lace curtains trimmed in purple, the walls nice grey color, and the bed was soft with purple satin sheets. I saw a flat screen TV on the wall; the floors marble.

Nurse: This room is where we put mothers to spend time with their newborn, but anyone can sleep here. So if you need anything just press that button over there.

Journey: Thanks.

So they transferred Honesty to the bed. I then laid on the other side keeping my eyes on her; but my eyelids started to get heavy, so I feel asleep.

Tuesday morning at 9:00 a.m., I woke up. I looked over to see how Honesty was doing, to my surprise she was not in bed. I jumped up to go look for her, and there she was staring out the window. She had a peaceful look on her face, yet her eyes were still closed. I slowly walked over to her and touched her shoulder, she just turned around and gave me a hug and I told her all is going to be okay. After I said that, she squeezed my waist; then the doctor walked in.

Dr. Smith: Well, well, I see you two are doing okay this morning. Journey: Yes, we slept well last night. This room is so beautiful.

Dr. Smith: Good to hear. Can you have Honesty sit down while I check her? Thanks. How would you say she is doing this morning?

Journey: I say she is doing better. When I woke up to check on her, she was up looking out the window. She had this peace about her.

Dr. Smith: Yes, there is, but I wonder how did she know a window is there? Anyway, before I let you go, I want you to order something to eat for the two of you; then we will go from there and it is on the house.

Journey: That sounds good, thanks, doc! It has been a while since we ate breakfast outside of the shelter.

The breakfast arrived; Honesty and I ate. She did well, but I had to help her find the food on her plate, after we were done, the doctor came back in.

Dr. Smith: Okay, I see you two ate well. I am glad to see Honesty doing better. I checked her eyes for the changing of colors you spoke on and found nothing. But as far as her eyes being black one moment then normal the next is something I've never seen or heard of. I could send her to an eye specialist, but that will take you having insurance.

Journey: Well, we have to apply for it.

Dr. Smith: Yes, and as I said, all tests were fine; over all she is healthy. Just don't let her give up on her drawing; there are blind schools. Oh, and to let you know that depression may set in; but if and when it does, she may act out, cry, or get angry. But keeping her busy will keep her mind off herself. Let me send in my nurse to get you going and give you some numbers to some resources.

Journey: Okay, Dr. Smith, thanks for everything.

Nurse: Okay, here are the phone numbers to get further help, and make sure you apply for insurance. Here are some shades for Honesty.

Journey: Thank you.

So I helped Honesty get dressed, then I called Jania.

Journey: (Dialing) Jania, hi, this is Journey. We're done, can you come get us?

Jania: Sure, I am on my way.

So Honesty and I sat in the waiting room, and while we were waiting Honesty did something strange. She pointed to a painting on the hospital wall. In shock, I whispered, "How did you know there is apainting there?" But she said nothing. I knew she wanted her paintingsupplies and that this was hard for her not being able to see. After twenty minutes, Jania walked up.

Jania: Are we ready! Well, this must be Honesty. Journey: Yes, this is my lovely daughter.

Jania: She's beautiful, and she has a pretty name.

Journey: Jania, before we go to your place, if it's all right with you, can we stop by the shelter? Our belongings are there.

Jania: Sure! Let's go.

I was happy that we met someone nice. Rarely you meet someone unexpectedly who wants to help you in a big city. So while we were riding, Jania and I talked a little. I told her how Honesty loved to draw and how she hoped one day to become a great sketch artist. Jania said to me that dreams do come true, and to make sure Honesty never gives up hope. We then arrived at the shelter; Jania came in with us.

The manager, Maleaka: My, my, Journey and Honesty, how are things going? Is Honesty okay?

Journey: Hi, Maleaka. Yes and no, but we are here to get our things. Sorry, let me introduce you. This is Jania, we met at the hospital. She overheard me telling the doctor how we would lose our bed if we were gone too long, so Jania asked me would we like to stay with her, and here we are. God is good.

Maleaka: That is wonderful. Nice to meet you, Jania, and God bless you for this act of kindness.

Jania: Well, thank you and nice meeting you. I must say you are doing a great job too helping the homeless.

Maleaka: Yes, it is wonderful to help others, but we are going to miss them both.

Journey: We will miss you too. Well I guess I will get our things. Since Honesty could not see, I led her to a chair to sit down while I packed our things, and Maleaka and Jania stayed with her.

Jania: Honesty and her mother had been through a lot since yesterday. It is so strange how things can happen unexpectedly, I guess you never know.

Maleaka: Yes, you are so right, but I hope Honesty will press on with her artwork. She is an awesome sketch artist.

Jania: Is she really? I'm looking forward to seeing her work; though she is blind, she can do it.

Maleaka: OMG! Honesty is blind? Journey did not tell me. This poor girl, I am sorry to hear this, Honesty.

Jania: I am glad I ran into them, but do not feel bad about them losing their bed. It is just company rules.

Maleaka: Ha, I was feeling rather sad, but thanks for the uplift.
Journey: Well, I got our things.

Maleaka: You got everything?

Journey: Yes, and thanks for being here for us, Maleaka. This is a wonderful place and I will tell others about it.

Maleaka: Well, you two take care and do stay in touch.

Journey: Honesty dear, can you wave bye to everyone? I guess she's not feeling well, goodbye to you all.

Finally, Honesty and I were on our way to a real home; but I still hope one day to get back on my feet so we wouldn't have to depend on anyone.

Jania: Well, in order to get to where I live, we will have to drive on to a ferry that will take about fifty-seven minutes. You will see lots of water, but it's a beautiful sight.

Journey: You picked us up fast; Seattle is so crowded. Jania: Oh, I was in the area closing a deal.

Journey: I see.

While I was sitting in the front seat, I turned around to see what Honesty was doing. To my surprise, she was drawing on her note pad. I asked her what was she drawing, she handed it to me and it was a toilet. It dawned on me that she needed to go to the restroom, but then I thought this was creepy because she can't see.

Jania: What did she draw? Journey: Ha, look.

Jania: Oh, my word. Is she saying she needs to go to the restroom? Okay, there is one right up here. Good job, Honesty! Wait, she is blind, how did she do that?

Journey: I do not know, maybe it comes natural.

So we stopped to let Honesty use the restroom. I walked her in. I was going to help her, but she shook her head no. I gave her some privacy and stood outside the door. She came out, and we got back on the road. I was still puzzled, and I know Jania was too as to how she drew that picture.

Jania: You know, even though she cannot see, looks like the other senses have sharpened. A person who becomes blind usually does not draw right away. This is strange to me.

Journey: I heard that saying too, but I pray that her sight comes back. She has a life ahead of her.

Jania: Of course, she does, and healing takes time. So have faith for her. Okay! Ferry time.

Finally, we had made it to Bainbridge Island. When we drove up to the house, it was so beautiful. I thought to myself, "Where am I." Water surrounded the homes, just beautiful.

Jania: Okay, this is it, girls! New home, new life. All will be better.

I said to Honesty, "Wow! This is a beautiful home," just to let her know how it looked, but the look on her face went blank again. She then walked slowly up to the house and stood there staring at it for about two minutes, but I did not know what she was thinking.

Jania: Oh, don't worry, Journey, she is just getting a feel of things. She will be all right. She cannot see, so that may be it. Let us put your things in the house. I can call my husband out to help us. Justice! Justice! Can you come and help us? Our guests are here.

Justice: Hello, I'm Justice! Pleased to meet you.

Journey: And I'm Journey and this is Honesty. Pleased to meet you.
Justice: I heard that Honesty is an artist.

Journey: Yes, she is and great at it.

Jania: Justice, you know what she did while we were driving? Without a single word, Honesty drew a toilet, which meant she had to go to the restroom, is that talent or what!

Justice: Yes, that is talent. Hey, maybe she can do some artwork in our guesthouse, you know, give her something to do.

Jania: Sounds good to me.

So we all headed into the house. Jania showed us the room Honestyand I would be sleeping in.

Jania: Here is the room. What do you think? Journey: It is lovely and roomy!

Jania: Honesty can sit her art stuff over by that big window that overlooks the island, just to give her some inspiration. Even though she cannot see, she can feel. Okay, girls, I'm going to settle in myself, and dinner will be ready at 5:00 p.m.

Journey: Jania, I want you to know you been a big help to us, and I hope one day I can repay you. Oh, I was going to ask you, are you okay?

Jania: What do you mean?

Journey: Well, you were at the hospital too.

Jania: Oh, I am fine. I was there to bring Dr. Smith his final papers to sign for the home he just bought. I must say I'm jealous because it is a nice home.

Journey: Ha, right, you are a realtor. Okay, see you soon.

So I started to put our things away, and Honesty was trying to fold her tops. In the middle of her folding, she stopped and started putting up her drawing equipment. I just stood there and looked at her for a moment how she was dropping things, but finally put up her canvas. I was thinking how can she do all this and she cannot see. When she was done she sat down to draw. I told her she could draw later when things are put away, but she just sat there. Then slowly she started to draw, so I stood back. She drew a face, but it had no eyes; then she drew the hair and the body. Then she stopped. I just continue to look at her, and then I walked up close to her ear and asked her what is wrong? Nevertheless, she just sat staring. Then she got up and continued folding her clothes which was strange too. She has never acted like this before. So when I was done putting things away, then there was a knock at the door. It was Jania. "Come in!"

Jania: I see you got things put away, just to let you know dinner is almost done. Oh I see, Honesty's been at work already, what is she drawing?

Journey: It looks like a person. Honesty likes to surprise me, she will not tell me, so I have to wait.

Both laughed.

Jania: Then a surprise it will be. Okay, I will meet you two downstairs.

I took Honesty by the hand so she would not trip, but she pulled away from me. I told her to let me help her, so she let me. We went downstairs; and when we got there, the table was set so lovely and we all sat down to eat.

Jania: Justice decided to cook dinner tonight for us. Journey: What is for dinner?

Justice: We are having pot roast, mashed potatoes, green salad, and ambrosia salad.

Journey: Smells good. I mean, the shelter served good food, but it is not like home cooking.

Jania: Well, you have a home-cooked meal now, so eat up.

So we all started to eat, and Honesty for some reason, kept staring at Justice. Then his cell phone rang.

Justice: Excuse me.

Jania: Justice always has business people calling him at dinner time and I hate it!

Then I looked over at Honesty, and she had her hands over her eyes as though something was wrong. She kept rubbing her eyes, and then I whispered in her ear and asked her what is wrong? She then yelled no, no, jumped up, and ran upstairs, bumping into the walls because she could not see.

Jania: OMG! What is wrong with her? she needs to go back to the ER.

Journey: No, I will go check on her, maybe her eyes are bothering As I was heading upstairs, Justice returned to eat.

Jania: Justice, who were you talking to? You have to start cutting your cell off at dinner time, too many interruptions.

Justice: Oh, that was a deal on a house. But you know how this goes, honey, I cannot miss money. Where are our guests? They haven't finished. Is everything okay?

Jania: I hope. Journey went upstairs to see if Honesty is okay; she was acting strange.

When I got upstairs I walked in the room, and Honesty was drawing. She had finished the picture so fast; I mean her speed increased. It was of a lady who was very pretty. I stood by her and said, "She's beautiful."

Then she dropped her paint brush. What was so weird about this photo is that she drew it without seeing this person. She then started to pace back and forth, and then a knock came at the door.

Jania talking through the door: Is everything all right?

As I was heading to the door to open it, Honesty ran to the door and blocked it. I told Jania to wait a moment. I did not know what Honesty was doing. She ran over to the drawing, picked it up, and hid it, and then came and stood by me. I couldn't believe what I just saw.

Jania, concerned speaking: Is Honesty okay?

Journey, opening the door: Huh, yeah, she's okay. I think she has just been through a lot. The hospital wore her out.

Jania: Well, I'm going to put the dinner away. If you need to finish your dinner, just heat it up in the microwave.

Journey: Okay, good night. Honesty, honey you need to lay down. So I got her dressed for bed, then we both lie down. As I lay there,

I thought about all Honesty and I had been through due to me losing my job, going from shelter to shelter; I prayed that one day my back would heal enough, so I could go back to work. It has been a long road for the both of us. I notice since Honesty became blind, I will have to keep an eye on her. I then fell asleep with all this on my mind. Before I knew it, it was 7:00 a.m., Tuesday morning. A knock came to the door.

"Come in!" I said. (Door opens) Hi, Jania. Jania: How did you sleep last night?

Journey: We slept well even though we didn't eat. But the bed was nice and soft and Honesty slept all night. Wow, what smells so good?

(Jania chuckles) Breakfast. As soon as you two get dressed, just come down, okay.

I told Honesty it was time to eat. We were used to getting up early, so we both got cleaned up and headed downstairs. When we got down there, everything looked and smelled good.

Jania: Well, I hope you two like wheat pancakes, scrambled egg, and turkey bacon because we don't eat pork; and we got fruit.

Journey: Sounds good. Let's eat.

(While I was eating, I notice Justice wasn't there) Is Justice coming to eat with us?

Jania: Huh . . . he had some business to take care of. He's always on the go with this deal and that deal; I'm sick of it.

Journey: Wow! I don't think I could handle a busy man like Justice.

Jania: Well, you kind of get use to it. Hey, I was thinking, after breakfast we should take Honesty over to the blind school so she can get some help.

Journey: Yeah, but we don't have money.

Jania: That's fine. I will pay for it, and then I can do a tax right off.

It's always nice to help people.

Journey: No, you have done enough already.

Jania: Honesty needs the help, so let's eat and we will go.

After we ate, around 9:00 a.m., I took Honesty upstairs, and when we got up there she took the unfinished picture and put it on the stand. She sat down. I told her we had to go somewhere, but she just sat there. Then she started to draw. I tried once again to tell her we had to go, but she kept on drawing. So I sat down and just looked at her draw. This time she drew the whole face, and when she got done she looked at it and started to point at it. I had no idea what she was trying to say; then she started to pace back and forth again. I grabbed her by the hand, but she pulled away from me. I didn't know what to think, she was acting so different. She went looking through the drawer and she found a pen and some paper, then she wrote something down. I looked at it and it said "the one". I said, "The one what?" But she just shook her head, "Never mind," and dropped the pen and paper on floor. Meanwhile, Jania was calling us. I told Honesty we had to go, so we went downstairs.

Jania: Is everything fine?

Before I could say anything, Honesty grabbed my hand and squeezed it as if she didn't want me to say anything. Knowing I hated lying I told Jania she was using the restroom. We got in the car and headed to the school. When we arrived, Jania said to let her do the talking. We went in and Honesty and I sat down.

Jania: Excuse me, who do I talk to about signing someone up for school?

Lady: That would be me.

Jania: Well, I have a friend here whose daughter, all in one day, became blind; therefore, she is going to need to learn braille. And she also is a sketch artist and I would like to know if there's a class to teach the blind to draw?

Journey: Umm, excuse me, Jania, she already draws, so she won't need that class.

Jania: Oh, okay. Just the reading class will be fine.

Lady: She draws blind? Amazing! Okay, yes we do have an opening. Just have the mother to fill these papers out and return them to me. Oh, and since she draws blind, we can put her in an art class as well to keep her inspired but we would have to do a pre-test to see where she stands. It will tell us how much work we need to do with her.

Jania: Okay, that's fine. Journey, here fill these papers out to the best of your ability, and when you get to the financial part, I will talk with the lady.

So I filled out the papers, then I left the rest up to Jania who's such an amazing person. I'm so glad I met her.

Jania: Okay, she's done.

Lady: Everything looks fine; and how is this going to be paid? Cash or check?

Jania: As her friend, I want to pay to put her daughter in school and I'm paying with cash.

Lady: Nice friend you are, not a lot of people would do this. Okay, that will be three thousand and that will cover three months.

Jania: Good, now when does she start?

Lady: Let's see, it is April so classes start July 1. Okay, follow me and we will see how well she does with her sketching.

Jania: I will wait here.

So we went to in the art room. I sat down and let Honesty focus. The lady stepped out. Then I saw Honesty pick up the pencil. She sat there for a few minutes, and then she started to draw. I notice she was drawing really fast, and she started getting upset. I told her to calm down, it's okay. But she shook her head no. Then she picked up the paint brush and she chose the color red. After she was done, it seemed like she was going to faint, so I ran over and held her up. As I looked over at what she drew, what I saw was terrifying. It was a picture of a female having an abortion, blood streaming down the page. So I helped Honesty over to the chair. Then I went over to the drawing and tore the picture down and balled it up, put it in water to rinse the paint off. Just as I was putting the picture in the trash, the lady walked in.

Lady: So let's see what she drew, oh, the page is blank.

Journey: Yes, she was feeling kind of faint, so she couldn't do it. Sorry.

Lady: It's okay. Maybe it's too soon; maybe next time. Jania: Okay, see you July 1st.

Lady: Bye now. (Lady talking to herself) Let me go clean this room and go home. What's this? Pieces of torn paper . . . hmm . . . and who used red today? The bottle is closed and the students today didn't use paint. Oh well.

Jania: Journey, in no time, Honesty will be reading braille. How did she do?

Journey: She didn't draw anything, but I will try and explain to her what this school is about. Let's see, it's April 9th, she doesn't have long.

Jania: Hey, I have not heard from my husband all day. I wonder if he's at the office. Before we go home, I will stop by his office to see if he wants to cook tonight.

So Jania stopped by the office. She went in. She was in there for about ten minutes. I reached down to pick up my purse, and when I looked up I could not believe my eyes. It was the woman Honesty drew. I was in shock. When I turned around to tell Honesty, she was already pointing at the woman. Then she started shaking her head saying no again. I remembered what she wrote on the paper, "the one," but I didn't know what that meant. Then Jania came out looking upset.

Jania: That Justice is getting on my nerves, he has another meeting tonight. Maybe we shouldn't have become retaliators.

Journey: Well, he's just trying to keep the good life. Look at what you two have now, would you rather live in a shelter?

Jania: Yes and no. At least if we were living in a shelter I would see him more; and no because we wouldn't have no money and I couldn't help people like you.

Journey: Aww, that's nice, but don't worry yourself I will cook.

Jania: You cook! (chuckles) Really?

Journey: Sure I do, but not lately, because I haven't had my own kitchen in a while.

So we headed home. I started to tell Jania how strange it was about the connection this woman had with Honesty's drawing. But before I could say anything, Honesty kicked under my seat. I never knew why my daughter wanted to keep her drawing of this woman a secret. So we arrived home and I asked Jania what she would like me to cook.

Jania: Cook whatever. There is plenty of food, I am going to lie down for a while. It's around 2:00 p.m., so we will eat at around five.

Journey: Five it is.

So Honesty and I went upstairs to get comfortable. When we got upstairs, she took out her picture to show me. I looked at her and said, "I know this is the woman." She then got the pen and paper and wrote the word "bad". Now I'm wondering what does this mean? And what was going on with Honesty and her drawing. I mean all this was weird and strange. Her drawing, knowing she can't see and drawing someone connected to Justice. I started to think, maybe my daughter needed to see a therapist, but I didn't have the money and I couldn't ask Jania because she's done too much for us already. So that left me to go to the state for help. Later, I told Honesty I was going to cook and for her to rest. I went downstairs; and while I was walking down, I overheard Jania talking to someone on the phone about church. She never appeared spiritual; so I continued walking to the kitchen to look for something to cook. I thawed out a couple of steaks, saw a barbeque pit and thought I would grill. I made a potato salad and some corn. Then Jania came down the stairs.

Jania: I smell coals, barbeque! I haven't had that in a long time.
Journey: Me either.

I thought to myself, should I start a conversation about church? But she said something first.

Jania: So, I was talking to my parents, they are pastors. They've been trying to get me and Justice to go to church, but he's not into it. I don't mind going; I've just been too busy.

Journey: Well, let's go together one day. Honesty and I used to go to Bible studies at the shelter, it was nice.

Jania: That would be okay. Besides, maybe you could speak with a pastor about Honesty's problem.

Journey: Yes, that's true. Maybe I can take her to see the pastor at the shelter, I need someone to talk to anyway.

Jania: Umm, Journey, just to let you know, if you ever want to go somewhere, you can drive one of the cars. And to save you from boiling the corn. I will do it Ha. I'll put it on for you, I can't rest anyway.

Journey: Thanks, Well you guys do have four cars (chuckles), and it's nice of you to offer. As a matter of fact, Honesty needs some better shades. And I do have license. Well, it won't be long before dinner is ready; I am going to go check on Honesty.

I headed up stairs to check on my daughter, and when I walked in she had drawn a picture of Justice standing next to the woman. I asked her, "Why did you draw Justice next to her?" I was not sure what this meant, I knew they work together and maybe that's what she was trying to say. But she kept pointing. I told her it was time for dinner and we will deal with this later; so we headed downstairs and Jania had dinner on the table and waiting. Out of the blue, Jania asked if Honesty has been drawing. I told her a little. She said she would like to see some of her work.

Jania: Hey, maybe she can draw a picture of Justice and I for our sixteenth anniversary.

Journey: I bet she could if she focused. Hey, how's dinner? Jania: You're a good cook!

Journey: Well, if Justice is too busy or going to be late getting home, I'll be glad to cook.

Jania: Sounds like a winner. You know, I cannot wait for Honesty to start school because then she will be able to communicate. She has not talked since this happened, right.

Journey: No, she hasn't talked; I cannot wait either.

By this time, Honesty had only finished half of her dinner. She got up from the table, and as she was going up the stairs, she had to touch the walls as a guide. I knew she was going to go draw, so I just left her alone. After dinner, Jania and I hung out and talked. She told me how she was upset because Justice was never home and how he always had houses to sell. However, I did not tell her about how Honesty's gift turned to be different or how my daughter was not the same, and I didn't know her anymore. I just couldn't share this with her. It has more to it; but if only Honesty could talk, I would not have to figure everything out. So after our little talk I headed upstairs to see what Honesty was doing. When I walked in this time, she was staring out the window. I walked over to her, and I turned her around and looked her in her eyes. She then pointed at the picture. I still did not understand why she was so adamant about the drawing. So I thought, since Jania said I could use one of the cars, I should get Honesty out of the house tomorrow.

Wednesday at 3:00 a.m.

(Honesty talking in her sleep, muffled sound) It is wrong. Why are you doing this to her? You're bad for her . . . leave . . . Go!

I heard Honesty mumbling; I think she was dreaming. So I shook her to wake her up. She just grabbed me and did not want to let go. I just lay by her all night.

At 7:30 a.m.

Jania knocking on door: Journey, are you up? Journey: Yes, I just finished getting dressed, come in.

(Door opens)

Jania: I was coming to tell you breakfast is ready. Journey: Okay, we'll be down.

So we headed downstairs, and when we got there, Justice's assistant, "the one", was at the table. It shocked me because I knew Honesty had drawn a picture of her.

Jania: Journey, this is Hymns; Hymns meet Journey. Both say nice to meet you.

Jania: Oh, and I cannot forget to mention who this beautiful girl is. This is Honesty, the sketcher. Ha.

Hymns: She sketches. Wow! How cool. Hi Honesty, nice to meet you.

When Hymns went to shake my daughter's hand, she just sat there with her head down, shaking her head no.

Journey: Sorry, she hasn't been feeling well.

Hymns: I understand. Mmmm, breakfast looks great, Jania. I must come by more often.

Jania: Anytime, Hymns, you have been a great secretary and a big asset to our business.

Hymns: Thank you!

Justice: I must say Jania couldn't have found a better person.

Hymns: Well, I'm thankful to both of you because I had just gotten out of college and I saw your ad. I called and we met and now I'm doing great. Thank you both.

I told Honesty to wait while I go get my purse because I was goanna take her for a ride. The weather wasn't bad, but I knew it rained a lot here so we carried a jacket. We then headed to the car when we got in the car, Honesty started to smile a little. This let me know she was happy about going for the ride, and plus, I hadn't seen her smile in a while. So I thought since we were out why not stop by the shelter we were in. This would surprise Honesty because she has friends there. But I had to go to the store first to get her shades. After getting off the ferry, I went to this store Honesty and I used to go to; and as we got close, she pointed in the direction the store was in. Letting me know that she knew where we were going. How she knew, I don't know. As we arrived at the store and she jumped out and just waited for me at the front door. I told her we we're there to get her shades.

Journey: Excuse me, miss, where are your shades?

Store lady: Over there to your right.

Journey: Thank you. Okay let's see here. Oh, these are nice, try these on, dear. Beautiful. I like them, let's get these.

So I got the shades and we left. I still didn't tell her we we're going to visit the shelter. Finally we arrived. When we pulled up, I looked at her face and she still had a smile, so we went in and there was a woman at the front desk.

Journey: Excuse me, is Maleaka working today? Lady: Yes, she is. May I tell her who is asking? Journey: Tell her Miss Brown and Honesty.

Lady: Okay, be right back.

Maleaka: OMG! Look who's here. Journey! Honesty! Give me a hug, how are you two doing?

Journey: We are doing great! God has been good to us. We now live with the lady you met and her husband; nice couple who lives in a big beautiful home. It is like heaven on earth.

Maleaka: Wonderful. And Honesty, you look pretty as ever. Come, let's go into the dining area. So tell me how is Honesty doing?

Journey: She's doing okay. The woman we live with was so nice that she paid for Honesty to go to a blind school.

Maleaka: That is a blessing. Would Honesty like to say hi to her friends?

Journey: You read my mind.

So I took Honesty by the hand and followed Maleaka. She took us to an area where the teens hang out. And when we walked in, three of Honesty's friends ran up to her and gave her a hug. Honesty was so happy that I let her go off and be with them for a while.

Maleaka: You girls watch her now. Let's sit over there. You know, I hope her sight comes back. I do believe in prayer and miracles.

Journey: I do too; but if her sight doesn't come back, she will have braille to fall back on. She still does her drawing, but since this happened to her she seems to have changed.

While I was talking, we heard screaming, one of Honesty's friends came running up to me, short of breath. She said Honesty needs our help. When Maleaka and I got to Honesty, blood was running down from under her shades. I told someone to get me a towel, and I tried to wipe her face, but it aggravated her more. She pushed me and I fell back.

Maleaka: Are you okay? OMG! You got to get her to the hospital. I'll call the hospital to let them know you are coming!

Journey: No! No! Please . . . I'll just take her there. Let me get her in the car. Sorry. I'll see you another time.

So I got my daughter in the car; and as I was driving, she threw her shades on the floor. Then she looked at me with those black bloody eyes, and something strange happened. As I kept glancing at her and driving, the blood went back up into her eyes. The blood was gone! I had to pull over because it scared me. So I parked the car, I took her by the hand, and told her I was taking her to the hospital. And as I went to pull off, in a low voice she said no, but to take her shopping. I was shocked because she never talked. I was speechless for a minute, then I told her she needed to go to the hospital and not shopping. She started to get angry and started hitting her fist on the car door. So I drove off and I found a mall and we went inside. We found a store and we went to the girl's section; and as I was looking at outfits, Honesty walked off. I went looking for her. She came up behind me with a black outfit;without any hesitation I bought it. Finally, we made it back home. Andas I was driving up, Jania was just going in the house.

It was 2:00 p.m. and late.

Jania: Did you two have fun?

Journey: (Stuttering) Umm. Yes . . . yes, we did. Thanks to the nicest woman in the world.

Jania: Oh, you don't have to say that.

Journey: I don't know how I will ever repay you, you have been like family to us. Oh, here is your change.

Jania: Keep it; and Justice is going to cook tonight. Isn't that a miracle?

Journey (chuckling): Well, that means I don't have to cook.

So we went inside, and I told Honesty I wanted her to go rest before dinner.

Jania: Hey, I see you got a bag, what did you buy?

Journey: I didn't get anything, but Honesty wanted this black outfit. She never liked black; all her clothes and her pictures was always full of colors.

Jania: Maybe it's a phase. Teens go through that.

Journey: Well, I hope you are right.

I'm tired, I need to relax; so I went up to do just that before dinner.

When I got to the room, Honesty was drawing. I sat down beside her and watched what she was going to draw next. After a few minutes, she started to draw a baby and I thought to myself, whose baby is this? Then she drew Justice and Hymns, and put the baby in Hymns arms. Not wanting to get into questioning her, I just told her the baby was pretty.

Jania: (knocking) Are you resting?

Journey: Not yet, come in. (Honesty stood by the pictures to hide it) (Door opens)}

Jania: I was thinking that if you ever needed to take Honesty to the doctor I would pay for it.

Journey: Oh no, Jania, you have done way too much. I can get medical.

Justice: (Passing by the room) Hey, you guys. How is Honesty coming along with her art? Don't forget our guesthouse needs some artwork.

Journey: Oh, she's doing well, drawing is something she loves.
Justice: How long has Honesty been drawing?

Journey: Since she was five years old. She would draw me nice pictures at school and bring them home to me.

Justice: Nice. Oh, my cell is ringing, excuse me. Hello, what! (Talking fades)

Jania: This is ridiculous. He always gets these calls that draw him away. I'm going to have a talk with him right now.

Journey: Don't be upset. Justice is a busy man and a hard worker.

Jania: I know; but when he is supposed to be making dinner and spending time with me, he should turn his phone off. So I am going to have a talk with him now.

I have never seen Jania upset. She jumped up and went to talk to Justice, and I got up to go downstairs to get something to drink. As I was heading downstairs, I saw Jania eavesdropping.

Justice's conversation: Hymns, how could you do this to me? You know we talked about you wanting to have my child which isn't a good idea. I thought you were taking birth control. Now you call me to tell me this outrageous message that you are pregnant. What do you mean you will not get an abortion? You have messed up. We will talk about this tomorrow at work. (Click)

As I stood back looking, when Justice walked out of his office Jania slapped him. I could not believe my eyes, but I continue listening.

Jania: How could you! After all that we have accomplished! And to top it off, you knew I couldn't have children. Yet you go and have an affair with Hymns who is twenty-eight and you forty-five years old and get her pregnant. I want a divorce!

Justice: Honey, listen! It is not what it seems, let's sit down and talk about this. You are making an irrational decision that you will regret later.

Jania: No! There is nothing to talk about. You had an affair and that's that. I knew these late night meetings and your cell phone ringing and being gone all the time were all a lie! I do not want to hear it! I want a divorce.

Justice: Listen, dear. Yes, I am wrong and I don't blame you for being angry, but we need to talk like adults.

I thought to myself, I'll just go back to the room because things were getting pretty hot. So I went upstairs. When I got to the room, Honesty was staring at the picture. I walked over and stood behind her to see who it was, and she still had Justice, Hymns, and the baby together in the picture. I could not believe what I saw. I looked at Honesty and she ran in the bathroom to hide. It came to me what Honesty was able to do; she's able to reveal hidden things. Later, I heard Jania's voice; she was coming up the stairs. My door was open, so I had to think fast where to hide the picture. Just as she walked up to the door, I grabbed the picture and pushed it under the bed; but I was a little late.

27

Jania: Journey, what are you sliding under the bed? Is that a picture? I have a better place for it.

Journey: (stuttering) Jus-just putting Honesty's drawing away.

Jania: Can I see it? At a moment like this, I need something beautiful to look at.

Journey: It's not complete.

And while I was talking, Honesty came out of bathroom and pushed it way under the bed with her foot.

Jania: Can I just take a peek, Honesty?

Journey: Umm . . . Honesty has this thing about her drawing, and that is she feels it's a jinx to show her drawing before it's complete. (Talking under breath) God, forgive me for lying.

Jania: Okay, show me later. (Started crying) Journey: Is everything all right, Jania?

Jania: No! And it never will be again. Can I talk to you in private? Journey: Sure. Honesty honey, I'll be right back. So where is Justice? Jania: Oh, he probably went to see her.

Journey: What is going on? Her who?

Jania: Well, Justice has been having an affair, and I'm not feeling so well. I want him out! I never thought he would do this to me. I mean, look at all we have; and now . . . it means nothing!

Journey: OMG! No . . . I'm so sorry, Jania. So now what?

Jania: I don't know. I mean, I love him and we been married for sixteen years, but he has to move. I have a headache. Do you mind going to the guesthouse? I have headache meds there in bathroom.

Journey: Sure, I'll take Honesty out there then she can see what it looks like.

(Jania talking to herself) There was something a little suspicious about Journey not wanting me to see that drawing. What could it be? Maybe it's me and Justice's anniversary picture, and I'm going to burn it! But I can stop guessing and go take a peek; let me see what she is hiding. OMG! What is this? This is Justice with Hymns and a baby, how did she know? And how can she draw so perfect when she can't see? Like what she did in the car. Are they a part of this? What does this mean? I will get to the bottom of this.

Journey (slamming the door); Jania, we're back!

I called her but she did not answer. I walked in the dining room and there she was holding Honesty's drawing.

Jania: Tell me, what is Honesty doing drawing a picture like this?

Journey: I-I can explain. Honesty honey, go upstairs. Let's sit down. You see, Jania, ever since Honesty had that unusual experience, she now has the ability to draw people she can't see and draw things that people hide. I don't know how she does it, but she can. I did not want you to see the drawing because I did not know how to tell you or if you would even believe me. I just found out myself what she can do.

Jania: Whoa! This is scary. I mean, I don't know if I believe you or if I want to. You hide it from me because you say you didn't know how to tell me, okay, I will try and believe this.

Journey: Like I said, you wouldn't believe me. Look, I'm not an interpreter but the picture speaks for itself.

Jania: There is a baby, Hymns is pregnant; I just found out. And you know what's so strange about this picture is that the baby isn't even born and she drew it.

Justice walks in the room.

Jania: Look what I got! You-you, sinner!

Justice: Who drew this? And why?

Jania: Honesty did. But it wasn't her drawing that revealed what you did, it's me overhearing you. Yeah, what's done in the dark will come to light!

Justice: (Stuttering) How-how did Honesty know? She must have seen Hymns somewhere.

Jania: (Sarcastically) Has she seen the baby too! She is blind, you fool.

Justice: This is crazy, how can this be? Is this some kind of magic trick! Is your daughter a witch! Or evil?

Journey: NO! My daughter is not a witch or evil. And I'm sorry but it's not Honesty's fault. She just has a gift, and since her accident she has been doing strange things; but we will go.

Jania: No! You stay; and before you get started, Justice, you have no right to blame these people. Why don't you get your stuff and get out! You are an adulterer; and don't try and turn this around. You are the cause of all this.

Justice: I'm not trying to turn this around; I'm just wondering how did Honesty know? Was she spying on us?

Jania: You are ridiculous. Once again, she can't even see, you idiot.

Justice: Something fishy is going on and I don't like it. I think them being here is going to make things worse, so maybe they should stay somewhere else.

Jania: I don't see anything wrong with them being here. I like her here and she may reveal something else.

Justice: All I'm saying, Jania, is that until we can get past what I did we do not need anyone around. They can come back when all this is over if that will make you happy.

Jania: Okay! Okay! But I will have to figure out where they will go. Maybe I will send them over to my friend Love. She has been going through a lot with Kavarri, it's contagious. And I think he moved out, so she could use some company, I will give her a call.

While I was upstairs packing our things, Jania knocked at the door.

Journey: Come in.

Jania: I'm sorry, Journey, but maybe Justice is right. It is much that I am going through, yet I would love for you and Honesty to stay. But I need to deal with Justice alone. I called my friend Love and she can use some company; so I will take you over there.

(At 5:00 p.m.)

So I got our stuff packed then we left. We drove for about forty-five minutes. We drove up to another big house. We got out of the car and we walked up to the door with Jania.

Jania rang the door bell.

Love: Jania, how you been? I haven't seen you in a while, come in.
Jania: It has been a while. Well, Love, I would like you to meet

Journey and her daughter Honesty.

Love: Beautiful names. Nice to meet you both, and welcome to Bellevue!

Jania: Thanks for helping me out. They are great people to have around. It's just that something came up with Justice, and I have to deal with it.

Love: Oh . . . I hope everything is all right. Whatever it is, don't take it too hard. You know, I and Kavarri went through a divorce and it's final. But think before you react. I regret it but then I don't.

Jania: I will and thanks, Love. Okay, girls, I will be in touch, and call me Journey if you need me.

Journey: Jania, can I speak with you? Jania: Sure.

Journey: Look, if you don't mind, please don't say anything to Love about Honesty's gift. I see it can start problems.

Jania: Oh no. I just told her Honesty is blind and that she is a great artist, but that's all I said.

Journey: Thanks, and I will miss you.

Jania: I will as well. (sniffing) They both hugged.

Love: Okay, let's get your stuff off the porch.

So Love helped bring our things in the house, then she showed us our room. It was another beautiful room. I asked her what she did for a living since she had such a nice home.

Love: Well, my husband Kavarri, who no longer lives here because we got a divorce, we had a contracting business. He had men who build homes. We had money problems, as in he wanted to control what goes in and what goes out. So I felt that if we wasn't going to be a team then we should get a divorce. So we sold the business, he ended up taking our daughter and giving me half and paying me spousal allowance.

Journey: Wow, I'm sorry to hear this.

Love: It's okay. It's 5:30 p.m. are you two hungry?

Journey: A little. And I don't know about my daughter, but if food is in front of her she might.

Love: Good, because I just ordered Chinese. Does Honesty like Chinese?

Journey: Yeah, she likes just about everything, and she's probably tired, but Chinese sounds good. So tell me how many rooms you have.

Love: Six and a pool.

Journey: You said you have a daughter?

Love: Yes, her name is Faith and she is fifteen. Journey: Does she come to see you?

Love: Yes, when she can sneak over or when her dad is with her. Journey: Oh, the father won't let you see her alone?

Love: No, he thinks I'm telling her bad things about him, so he prefers to be with her when she comes to see me.

Journey: You look young, how old are you?

Love: I'm forty and Kavarri is forty-four. And you are? Journey: I'm forty-one and Honesty is thirteen.

Love: I heard Honesty is an artist, what are her favorite things to draw?

Journey: She doesn't have a favorite. She draws everything and anyone. She started out really young.

Love: Well, she's going to have to draw me something one day. I'm not for sure how long Jania wanted you to be here, but it doesn't matter because I can use the company.

Doorbell rings.

Love: It must be the food. (opens door) Hello, here you go and keep the change.

Delivery boy: Thank you! Journey: Smells good.

Love: Oh yeah, they have excellent food. I rarely cook anymore.

Journey: Seems like you and Jania are in the same boat. She doesn't cook either, but I cook; so there you have it, no more eating out.

Love: Ha, I now have a build in cook, great!

So I fixed Honesty's plate and I put the fork in her hand then we all sat down to eat. I was really comfortable being around Love. She was pretty, slim, and she dressed nice. After dinner I took Honesty upstairs to rest, then Love and I sat and watch TV until she got a phone call.

(At 6:30 p.m.)

Love, on phone: Hello! Oh you decided to call, are you bringing Faith to see me? What you mean you don't know? Then figure it out. Are you seeing a woman? Oh yeah right, you're single, whatever. Let me talk to her. Hi dear, how's school? Oh, you're still on the honor roll, great! Well, I hope your dad will bring you over this weekend. Let's see, today is Monday, so maybe Saturday he should bring you over. (Whispering to Faith) Listen, don't forget to meet me for lunch tomorrow. We do this every day, and don't forget to call me to say goodnight before you go to bed, like we do every night. Love you, dear. Bye.

Journey: Was that your ex-husband?

Love: Unfortunately, yes. He tells me he is not seeing anyone, but I think he is.

Journey: Well, do you care if he does?

Love: A little. Only because I want to make sure whoever he is with, that she is treating Faith right. You know how those wicked girlfriends can be.

Journey: Yeah, they can be pretty nasty. Can you call Faith?

Love: No, because he is a jerk, but I'm thinking about getting her a cell phone. I can call her when I want to, but she can't let her father know.

Journey: Smart thought. But are you sure she won't tell?

Love: No, she won't tell. She hates the fact that her father doesn't let her come over by herself, so she has to sneak. I just wish we could resolve all this mess.

Journey: Well, just pray about it. That's what got me through.

Besides, look at all you have; are you not happy?

Love: No, I'm not happy. But if my daughter were here, I would be happy and less angry. I do know that money isn't everything, but we need it to live.

Journey: True, because if I had money I could have put Honesty and I in a home and not had lived in a shelter. But soon Faith will be able to make her own decision and no one can say anything.

Love: I don't mind him seeing anyone, but he doesn't have to lie about it; and if I find out he has lied, I will start a war. Anyway I am going to lie down. It's 7:00 p.m.

Journey: Okay, get some rest.

So I went to check on Honesty. When I walked in the room, she was on the bed with her face in the pillow. I ran over to turn her over, but she started to fight back as though she didn't want me to touch her. I was calling her name and shaking her but it was as if she couldn't hear me. Finally I got her to turn over. It looked as though she had been dreaming. Then I sat by her and she gave me a hug. I notice she was sweating, so I went and got a cloth to wipe her face. Later she went over to draw. I left her to herself. I went outside on the deck to get some fresh air. I sat in a rocking chair. I must have fallen asleep because I woke up to Honesty shaking me. I said, "Yes, honey." Then she just grabbed my hand and took me to the room. I looked at what she drew. When I looked, it was a drawing of a man standing by a plane with a young girl. I told her how pretty the picture was, but she shook her head no. I asked what she meant by no? She just started pacing. She paced for two minutes then she lay down.

A week later, at 6:00 p.m.

Love: Something strange is going on. Usually Faith calls me around this time to tell me good night, but I have not heard from her.

Journey: Really?

Love: Well, I can't call her school because he fixed it that if I call her school they would call him. I think I better get her a cell phone like I said.

Journey: Well, sooner or later you'll hear from her. Just try and relax.

Love: Or I can go by his house while he is at work, and be there when Faith gets home from school.

Journey: Would that be all right, I mean would you get in trouble?

Love: I don't know and I don't care. Hey, will you ride with me over there tomorrow?

Journey: Sure I'll go.

Love: Faith gets home around 2:30 p.m. We will meet her then.

Well, I'm going to bed early tonight. Sleep well.

Journey: Okay, have a good sleep.

The next morning, about 9:00 a.m., we ate breakfast, and we all got dressed. I did some cleaning up our room and washed some clothes. While I did chores, Honesty kept staring at the picture she drew with the plane. Then she put her hands over her ears and started yelling no, no! So I dropped what I was doing to see after her. In that same moment, Love passed by our room.

Love: Is everything okay? I heard Honesty yelling. Journey: She's fine. I think her eyes hurt her sometimes.

Love: Oh, how sad. She has to go through this. You can stay here and I can go by myself to see Faith.

Journey: No, I will go with you. Honesty will be fine Love: Okay. (shuts the door)

(At 2:00 p.m.)

Love: Journey! I'm ready.

Journey: Okay! Let me get Honesty.

So I went back in the room to get Honesty; and as I was walking in, she was holding the picture she drew of the plane. I told her we had to go, but she just stood there. I told her to snap out of it because Love was waiting and I didn't want her to get suspicious. I took the picture away and grabbed her hand. As we were heading out the door, Honesty started to point at the picture, and it came to me that she was trying to tell me something again. I took her to the side and I looked her in her eyes. I asked her, "What are you trying to say?" She then went over and grabbed the picture and brought it over to me. She had a look on her face that lets me know she had one of her vision. So we got downstairs and I called Love.

Journey: Hey, you say you are going over there? Well, I think you should call the police first.

Love: Why? I don't need to call them.

Journey: Since you told me you haven't heard from your daughter, that seemed kind of weird to me. For some reason I feel something is not right. Let's stop talking and get over there.

So we finally left and Love was speeding. The look she had on her face when I told her that was a look of terror. While she was driving, all of a sudden we came to a stop.

Love: There's his home. (Speaking sarcastically) Oh, look how nice his home is, and he didn't want to pay child support. That's why he took her.

37

Journey: I don't see any car.

Love: He keeps his four cars in a back garage. Hey look! Who is that inside?

Journey: It's a lady. Who could that be, his girlfriend? Love: No, she's too plain looking. I'm going up there.

Honesty and I waited in the car Honesty tapped on my shoulder, trying to tell me something. I asked her what she wanted. She started pointing at the woman, but I didn't understand what she was trying to say. When I turned around, Love was running back to the car.

Love: (Out of breath) Oh, my God! Oh, my God! Journey: What is it! Who is that woman?

Love: He moved. My-my daughter is gone and he hired that cleaning lady. Where's my cell, I got to call the police. Wait, you said that didn't you? Are you one of those people who can see things, feel things?

Journey: No, but calm down. If you are panicking they will not understand you.

While Love was on her cell outside the car, Honesty was in the backseat starting to become restless, moving back and forth, and then she let out a scream. I jumped and Love opened the car door to see what was wrong.

Love: (whispering) Is she okay?

Journey: She's just having one of her episodes.

I got out of the car and opened the back car door and sat in the back with Honesty.

Love: Hello! I'm calling to report a kidnap. It's my daughter, Faith Robinson. She's been missing for a week. No, she lives with her father. Can you send an officer out? My address is 1418 W Lake Sammamish Pkwy N.E Bellevue. Okay, thanks. Let's get back to the house.

Journey: How is that she is missing when he has custody?

Love: Because when we divorced, it was stated that he was not to move anywhere without letting me know. If he did, he would be in contempt of court.

Later we arrived at the house. When we drove up, the officers were there.

Love: Good they're here. Hello, Officers. I'm Love and I called you, and this is my friend Journey. Please come in.

Officer Andrews: I'm Officer Andrews and this is my partner Officer Byrd. So you said your daughter is missing? What makes you think this?

Love: Well, she lives with her father. When we got a divorce, it was stated that if he moved he was to notify me. So I went to his home today and it's empty.

Officer Andrews: When was the last time you heard from your daughter?

Love: It's been a week now.

Officer Byrd: Have you checked her school? Love: I can't without his permission.

Officer Byrd: And what is your ex-husband's name? Love: Kavarri Robinson.

Officer Andrews: And how old is Faith? Love: She's fifteen.

Officer Byrd: Do you have photos of them both?

Love: Sure. Let me get them. Okay, these were taken two weeks ago. Officer Byrd: Beautiful girl. We will need to take them with us.

Also, is there any place that you think he may have gone?

Love: No. He travels to many places; none that stands out. Officer

Andrews: Well, if you remember anything or hear anything, give me or my partner a call. Here's our card. Take care.

Love: Okay, thanks. Bye.

Journey: This is sad. Why would he do this?

Love: I have no idea, but it's obvious he's been plotting this move. My God! I can't live like this. I mean, I should have taken her with me after the divorce. Huh.

Journey: Just relax. Sit down and let me make you a cup of tea.

Love (crying) Oh, you are so blessed to have your daughter with you.

Journey: Yes, I am. Her dad, Jeremiah, just disappeared on us, so I never had to deal with him trying to take her. After Honesty was born, four years later, he said he had a job offer out of town that was making big money. After he left, I never saw or heard from him. Here sip this tea.

Love: That was horrible what he did. Thanks. Green tea, my favorite. I'm so pooped. I hope Faith calls. She knows I'm worried, and he knows how this hurts me.

Journey: Of course, she knows. I'm going to go check on Honesty.

She went to her room while the officers were here.

Love: Wow, it's 5:00 p.m., time flies. Go check on her, and I'll just sit back and hope Faith calls me. I'm sure there are leftovers; I'll find something.

Journey: Okay, and I'll find something later.

I went to check on Honesty. When I got to the room, she wasn't lying down; she was drawing again. I walked over to see what she was drawing. This time it was a drawing of green trees surrounded by water. She looked at me with a blank look on her face. I told her it was beautiful. So I went to walk away, but she grabbed my hand. I turned back around and looked at the picture again. I didn't catch on to what she was trying to tell me. The drawing didn't have anyone in it, so I didn't feel anything was wrong. Then she started to pace the floor. I told her to calm down because I saw she was getting upset. I suggested she lie down while I went back to check on Love.

Love: How is Honesty doing?

Journey: Oh, she's fine. Well, it's getting late and you haven't even rested.

Love: It's hard to, I just need some answers. It's very painful to go through this. I don't understand why he is doing this.

Journey: I can't imagine.

Love: Im going to see my lawyer Semaj tomorrow. I need to talk to him about all this.

Journey: Good idea. I'm going to turn in early. I think I'll make a sandwich for me and Honesty and let that be it. Just want to get some sleep.

Love: Sure, goodnight.

The next morning at 9:00 a.m., Love is in the kitchen.Journey: I thought I smell coffee.

Love: Morning. I didn't cook breakfast because I'm heading over to my lawyer's office.

Journey: That's okay. I know how to cook.

Love: Okay. I will be back; and if any strange calls come in, call me. Got to go. (shuts door)

So I just sat down and had some coffee. Ten minutes later, the phone rang. Journey: Hello! Who? I can't understand you! (Click) Hmm. They

41

hung up. (speaking suspiciously) Who was that? I went to turn around and Honesty was there.

Honesty: (in a small soft voice) It was faith.

Journey: Oh, Honesty, you startle me! You talked! You haven't talked since your accident. Oh, my God! Do you know where Faith is? Tell me!

But she just shut down as if she never talked. So I called Love. (cell ringing)

Love: Hello! Hey, Journey, what! Did a number show up on the caller ID? I'll be right there as soon as I get done.

After I hung up the phone, I turned around to talk to Honesty but she was gone. I went to the room. When I open the door, Honesty was drawing again. I said, "Honesty honey, I know you are blind and this is hard for you, but you got to stop walking off. I know you know something. I looked at your drawing, but it just didn't look like nowhere here.

(Door slams)

Love: Journey! I'm here.

Journey: Honesty, let me go talk to Love. I see you made it! Well, all I know is whoever called was whispering, and they sounded far away and it was a bunch of static.

Love: It probably was Faith! Did a number show up on the caller ID?

Journey: No, but you should call Officer Andrews or Byrd.

Love: Yes, I should. (Dialing) Hello, this is Love Robinson. Is Officer Andrews or Byrd in? Okay, can you have one of them to call me? They have my number. Thank you. (click) Well, I talked with my lawyer, Semaj, and it still stands that my ex-husband was to let me know if he was going to move. It was agreed between him and I that he could keep her for the simple fact that we didn't want to transfer her to a new school because she had friends and involved in sports and on the honor roll.

But I'm thinking Faith is trying to reach me.

Journey: Well, let's not jump to conclusion. (Phone rings)

Love: Hello, yes, this is Love. Hi, Officer Andrews. Well, I was calling you because my friend received a strange phone call while I was out. She said that the person on the other end was whispering and it was a lot of static in the background. No, no number showed up. Oh, that'll be great. Sure, I'll be here. Okay, bye.

Journey: What did he say?

Love: Well, he's going to come over and tap my phone. That way if she calls again it will pick up where she is.

Journey: I know this is hard for you, but you must pray to calm down and keep your sanity.

Love: I never was a praying woman and neither was my husband a praying man. My mother and father who passed away four years apart, they periodically would mention going to church. But that was because someone at her work was a Christian and would invite her to service, but we never went. So I never really understood it, how prayer worked, but I know it doesn't hurt to and at this point I can try it.

Journey: Yes, you sure can. Do you have siblings?

Love: Yes, her name is Hope, and she lives in Olympia, Washington with her husband Denali. They have no kids and they both are college professors at a university. She's older than me, she's forty-eight.

Journey: Do you ever talk to her?

Love: Not really. We email or text every now and then but not enough to tell her what's going on in my life. And she doesn't tell me what's going on in her life either. (knock knock)

Officer Byrd: Hello again. I got this device to hook to your phone, shouldn't take long. Tapping phones has been a great asset for law enforcement and it's pretty reliable. Just let me hook it to the phone and it will be ready to start processing calls.

Love: Well, I hope she calls back, I mean it's been very hard to not see or talk to her. (crying) He knows how much this hurts me, yet he acts like he doesn't care. I knew I should have kept her home with me, she always wanted to be with me.

Officer Byrd: I understand. I have children too, and I couldn't imagine my wife doing something like this. anyway it's done. Just let the system do its job.

Love: Thank you so much. Bye. Thank God. Now I hope she calls. This way he would get caught and my daughter will be back home with me.

Journey: You haven't been looking so good, why don't you take a nap? It's 2:00 p.m.

Love: Sounds good, but I have to check my store. Journey: You have a store?

Love: Oh, I didn't tell you. Well, after the divorce, with the money he gave me, I opened up a small gift shop across town. It's doing well. I call it FAITH'S GIFT SHOP".

Journey: OMG! Why you never told me? I mean is it a secret?

Love: No, just didn't say anything; too much going on, but I opened it with Faith in mind. She loved sending gifts to friends and family. So I thought I open a store, and when she turned eighteen she could run the shop and save up for a car she wanted.

Journey: So do you work at the shop?

Love: No. I have a college graduate working for extra money to pay off her student loans.

Journey: That's great! Do you need more help?

Love: Yeah, I could use some help. The shop is opened four days a week because she has another job. My hours are 9:00 a.m. to 5:00 p.m., but it would be nice to be open Fridays and Saturdays to sell more things. So while she is at her other job, the two days can be yours if you want it.

Journey: Really! I haven't worked in I don't know how long. I hurt my back one day at home. I was up on a chair trying to get my china and I lost my balance and fell. So I had to have back surgery. After the surgery I didn't return back to work, so I lost my job which led to me not being able to pay my bills. That's what landed us in the shelter. I miss working at the court house.

Love: Does your back hurt now?

Journey: Well, sometimes, but I can do light duty stuff and a little standing.

Love: I have some things that need to be filed, and you could do that while Mercy works on the floor.

Journey: Her name is Mercy.

Love: Cool name. Let's take a drive over there, it's getting late and we can get something to eat on the way home.

So I went upstairs to get Honesty, then we left. I thought I would never get a job; I'm so thrilled, but my concern was my daughter. I would have to keep an eye on her all the time. After a twenty-minute drive, we arrived at the store.

Love: Here it is; let's go in. Journey: Nice location.

When we got inside, the carpet was back. The walls were a lavender color, incense burning. I heard soft music playing.

Love: Hi Mercy! How are things going here?

Mercy: Fine and how have you been? You don't come in that often, but as you see, I've been keeping it up.

Love: I've been busy, and since I haven't been up here in a while, I decided to stop by with a friend of mine. Journey, meet Mercy. (Both said nice to meet you) And this is her beautiful daughter, Honesty. I came by to show them around because she and I were talking about you having help in the store, and how it would be nice to be open on Fridays and Saturdays.

Mercy: That would help bring in more profit too, it's great! Ooh, customers, got to go.

Love: Journey, come back here to my office. Okay, these are the papers that need filing. Every year I have customers who I call to tell them about new merchandise. And this is our new stuff here, so you would call them and tell them about the merchandise.

Journey: Wow! Getting back to work feels good. But will it be okay for Honesty to come here with me?

Love: Sure, it's fine. She can bring her art stuff and sit back here in the office. Okay, let's go now. Mercy, you're doing a great job, but call me if you need me for anything. And put the sign up saying OPEN FRIDAYS AND SATURDAYS; and since tomorrow is Friday, Journey can come in.

Mercy: Okay and nice meeting you both.

As we were walking out, Honesty stood staring at Mercy. I told her to come on but she just stood staring.

Mercy: She must like me. (smiling)

Journey: Yeah, she's very friendly. (smiling) Okay, Honesty, we got to go.

So we headed back home, and on the way, Love stopped at a Mexican restaurant to get dinner. Honesty and I waited in the car. I thought to myself, why was Honesty staring at Mercy?

Love: Okay, girls, I got some good Mexican food.

Journey: Sounds good. Hey, how long have you known Mercy?

Love: Well, I knew her for a year now. She is a hard worker. I met her through Kavarri. The two of them went to the same college. He was taking some classes on Business Management and she happened to be in his class. Somehow they became friends and he found out she was looking for work, so I hired her.

Journey: That worked out just fine. She seems to be well organized.

Love: Yep, she is a really big help. I mean I have so much going on at that store that there was no way I could have ran it on my own.

Journey: Well, I'm so thankful you offered me a job and I will do my best to help you.

So we arrived home and I took Honesty to the room to get washed up, but she pointed to her painting as if to tell me she wanted to do some drawing. So she went over and sat down to finish where she left off. I just went down to the living room so she could do her drawing.

(Love on the couch looking out her big bay window)

Journey: It smells good.

Love: Yes, it does. Help yourself and make Honesty a plate. I'll eat later.

I made me and Honesty a plate then I took her plate to her. When I walked in, she was still drawing. I laid the plates down, then I walked over and she had drawn this beautiful lady standing by Mercy. I told Honesty that she can't be drawing people she don't know. Then she grabbed my hand. I asked her what she's trying to tell me, but she sat there. I had no clue as to why she was drawing these people.

Love: Journey!

Journey: Stay here and eat. Coming!

Love: I wanted to ask you, do you think you can really work, I mean will it be too hard on you.

Journey: I feel I'm ready. I feel pretty strong. Love: How's Honesty doing?

Journey: She's fine. She's just trying to process all that has happened to her, and I know it will take time to get through.

Love: I know it's hard. I mean all that has happened. And I hope Jania is doing fine too. Have you called her?

Journey: No, but I should. It's really sad how people cheat on their mates.

Love: Or run off with your daughter. Sorry, I'm so mad. (crying)

Journey: Don't cry, it will be all right. Let's pray. Lord, we thank you for the food and our health. Lord, please bring Faith home, her mother really would like her home safe and unharmed. Amen.

Love: Nice prayer, thank you. Well, it's getting late. I'm gonna eat a little then go to bed.

Journey: Sleep well, and don't worry. Next morning at 8:00 a.m.

Love: Journey! I'm back. (door slams) Journey: Where have you been?

Love: Out, doing some banking. I ran into Jania and she said she hopes you really decided to take Honesty to that blind school.

Journey: Well, I don't know if she should go. I mean it may be too much at this time, and I'm sure the school will give her money back.

Love: Well, call Jania and talk to her about it. I wonder where my Faith is, I miss her; and you have to be at the store.

Journey: I know you do, I know I can't help much but try and pray.

Okay. I'm dressed for work.

Love: Let's go at noon; Mercy is there.

Journey: Okay, I'll give Jania a call. (ringing) Hello, Jania! How are you? This is Journey. I'm calling because Love told me she ran into you. I called to say that I don't think at this time Honesty should go to school.

Jania: Oh, really? It doesn't have to be on that date.

Journey: Oh, I see. So you will call the school. Great! Thanks for all your help. How are you and Justice? What you mean you put him out! He moved in with Hymns? Oh, I'm so sorry to hear this. Well, I'm going to stay in touch with you, okay and don't hesitate to call me.

Jania: Okay. Bye. Journey: Bye.

Love: Sounds like things got worse for her.

Journey: Yes, Justice moved out and in with that Hymns girl. How horrible. Oh, she said that whenever I think Honesty is ready for school I could just take her. She also said she will call them to explain our situation.

Well, I'm going to go upstairs and check on Honesty. Love: Okay, I'll just rest.

Journey: Okay.

So I went upstairs to check on Honesty. When I walked in, she was pacing back and forth. I grabbed her hand and she pulled away. Seems like she was frustrated about something but I didn't know what. So I grabbed her hand. this time I held tight and sat her down. I asked her what was wrong with her. But she just sat with a blank look on her face. I then walked over to the picture she drew. I wanted to know who the other woman was and if Love knew her too. I didn't know if I should show it to Love because she didn't know about Honesty's gift, and I didn't want what happen in Jania's house to happen in this house. I was between a rock and a hard place, but I knew I had to get to the bottom of this.

At 7:00 a.m., just waking up, Love was in the kitchen, in her red silk robe, yelling at the bottom of the stairs

Love: Journey dear! Coffee is done if you want some.

Journey: Okay! Just got out of shower, be down. While Honesty was in the tub, I got dressed, made the bed, and then went back in to check on her. When I walked in the bathroom, what I saw was horrifying; the tub was full of blood. I thought she had cut herself, but it was her eyes. They're bleeding so bad that the water turned red. I was hoping Love didn't come up while I cleaned up. So I just got her a towel and dried her off really fast. Then I cleaned the bathtub. I didn't know why her eyes were bleeding like that, and taking her to the hospital was pointless. So I just got her dressed and combed her hair. I couldn't believe how long it grew, it seemed like her hair was also turning black since this happen to her. Then I bagged the bloody towels and hid them so I could wash them later.

Love, walking up stairs: Journey! Journey: Come in!

Love: Well, you both look nice. Journey in your black skirt and boots and Honesty in her new black dress. Umm, are you going to eat before you go?

Journey: Yes, it takes a bit to help Honesty get herself together. Love: I understand. Well, no phone calls yet, and this is killing me.

Journey: I'm sorry, but you must keep praying to stay grounded.

Don't give up on that.

Love: Well, I'm going to get dressed, and we can leave at 8:40 a.m. Journey: Sounds good. Honesty, let's go eat.

We went downstairs and I fixed us breakfast. While I was cooking, Honesty walked around and touched things to feel her way through the house. She then went over by the bookcase; she touched things that sat on the fireplace. She then walked over to Love's photo gallery. She ran her fingers over a few books, then picked up a photo album. I sort of lost concentration; I was looking at her to see what she was doing. She then opened the photo album, she flipped through it, and she stopped on a photo. In a still small voice she said, "Hope" then laid down the album and felt her way back to the kitchen. I was in shock because Honesty never talks; I mean it's far in between. So I went back into the kitchen and continued making our plates, then Love came down in a nice red and black skirt and black heels.

Love: Smells good! Ooh, it looks nice out today here in Bell town. I'll be so glad when August comes because that's when I open the other side of my store.

Journey: What other side ?

Love: Oh, I didn't tell you, did I? Well, it's a consignment shop where people bring their clothes, shoes, and jewellery for me to sell, and I get percentage off it. But what I like about it most is that the clothes are from the wealthy.

Journey: Nice. So I could work back there when it opens?

Love: Sure. Hey, my sister text me on my cell. Funny she asked how Faith was. I never told her about what's going on, I just don't want her to know.

Journey: Why?

Love: Because we don't talk and I don't want to involve her in my life. We never were really close growing up. We both encouraged one another to achieve our dream, but that's as far as it went.

Journey: That's sad. Well, you never know what may happen in the long run. Somehow you two may come together one day.

Love: Well, we will see. Let's go.

So we left. When we arrived at the store, people were outside waiting for the store to open. I've never seen so many people waiting for a store to open.

Love: Look at them. This is going to be a great Friday. Let's go through the back. Oh, and Mercy is here because I needed her to help open up, but she is going to her next job at noon.

We went in and Mercy opened the doors and Love greeted the shoppers. It seemed like a nice place to work.

Love: Hi, everyone. If this is your first time here, then welcome to FAITH'S GIFT SHOP. As all of you can see, I will be open Fridays and Saturdays. Enjoy your shopping.

Journey: Love, can I see you for a sec? Umm, where do you want me to start?

Love: Oh, sure, follow me. Let's see, in this file cabinet are old customers who need to be put in order. When you are done with that task then you can call them and tell them about our new arrivals.

Journey: Great! I'll get right on it.

I started filing and Honesty sat drawing. It was a lot of customers to file, but I was use to it. While I was filing, Mercy came in to see how we were doing.

Mercy: Hey! How are you doing back here? Journey: Well, let's put it like this, I love it!

Mercy: Good! Glad you like it. You know, I was looking at Honesty's hair and I wondered where she gets her black silky hair from because I see your a brownie.

Journey: You know, I wonder that too because her dad's hair is dark brown, and my mother's hair was like a reddish color and my father has brown hair. So yeah, I wonder.

Mercy: Wow, I wish I had hair that went past my butt. Anyway I'll be in the front if you need me.

Journey: Okay.

So I got back to filing. When Mercy walked out, Honesty pointed at her. I told Honesty not to point because it wasn't polite. But she kept pointing, so I stopped what I was doing to go put her finger down. But when I touched her hand, it was cold as ice, as if it was frozen. So I ran quickly to the rest room to see if I could find something to run warm water on, and I found a towel. I got it warm, then I went to put it on her hand. But when I returned, she was sitting and her hand was warm to touch. I looked at her in shock. I asked her, "What is going on with you?" But she did not respond. I asked Honesty why she was pointing at Mercy with a mean look on her face. I squat down in front of her to get close to ask her, but she jumped up and went and stood in the corner. While she was standing there, Love walked in.

Love: Hey! {voice fades} girls, why is Honesty in the corner? Is she in trouble? Isn't she too old for time out?

Journey: Well, there is one little detail I didn't tell you. When Honesty stands in a corner, she feels she is hiding from any trouble she may feel is happening in her mind. A corner is like a safe place.

Love: Oh, okay. I don't get it but okay. So how are you doing?
Journey: I'm doing fine, look.

Love: Wow! You are good, you are a keeper. Well, I'll let you continue.

Journey: Bye.

When Love walked out, Honesty turned around and said in a low voice, "You lied." I said surprisingly, "Honesty, you talked again." I told her yes, I did lie as to why she was standing in the corner and that I was sorry, but that's so I didn't have to explain what I just witness. After I said that she just went and sat down and started drawing. I finished all the filing then

I took a break. I went out to the front and there were more customers. So I got some coffee and just looked around.

Love: Journey! Glad you are taking your break?

Journey: Yes, it's noon. Wow! You got people all over this store. Love: Yep, and thanks to you, we can be open two more days. Journey: My pleasure. I'm going to get back to work.

Love: You didn't even take thirty minutes, but okay, I'll be in front if you need me because Mercy is gone now.

Journey: Okay.

So I went to the back to ask Honesty if she was hungry or thirsty, but she said no. So I started on another pile. Then Honesty came over to show me what she drew, and I looked. It was a two story home. It was beautiful and I told her it was. She pointed to a name she wrote and it said Mercy. I asked her if it was Mercy's home. She shook her head no and went and sat down. I just continued doing my work. Then Mercy came in because she forgot something.

Mercy: Wow! This looks so neat, how did you do it?

Journey: Well, I was a file clerk at the courts for so long it comes natural. I hurt my back at home so that ended me working. And as I was talking, Honesty got up and stood by Mercy.

Mercy: Hey, Honesty, how are you doing? How is your drawing coming along? Can I see what you drew today?

Honesty shook her head no.

Journey: She's funny about showing people her drawings, I don't know why; but she must like you because she never stands by anyone.

Mercy: Then that's a good thing. Well, I forgot my purse back here, got it. I'm going to go and I won't be here tomorrow which is Saturday, so the store is all yours.

Journey: Save me. (chuckles) Have a nice day. Mercy: Thanks, bye.

Journey: Wow, time is flying.

So I started calling old customers; and while I was doing that, Honesty started to pace back and forth. She would stare at the house she drew. Then Love walked in.

Love: We did it! We sold all kinds of gifts today. My money is working for me. Faith is going to have a great store when she turns eighteen. (crying) Oh, Faith, where are you? Call me, please.

Journey: Look, this is too much for you to be here. We only got two more hours, so why don't you just sit back here and let me run the front.

Love: Oh, okay, I guess. No, it is 4:00 p.m.; we got one hour, I'll just rest.

So I ran the front and it was busy, but I made it through. We locked up and went home. We arrived home around 6:00 p.m. due to traffic. When we got home, all of us got undressed and comfortable. I was hungry, so I made Honesty and I something to eat. I noticed my daughter's appetite had changed since she became blind. I asked Love if she wanted to eat. She said yes, so I made soup and turkey sandwiches. It was a long day, then the phone rang.

Love: Hello! Hello! Who is this? Who? I can't hear you. (click)

Journey: Who was that?

Love: I don't know. I couldn't hear them. Kind of like the call you got.

Journey: Go look at the machine the police left.

Love: Well, it shows the area is in Florida, but unknown number. I don't know anyone in Florida.

Journey: (talking to herself) I know Honesty knows something, but

I can't tell Love that she knows. And I remember Honesty saying to me that that last call was Faith.

Love: Journey! Journey! I'm talking to you. Journey: Yes . . . yes, what did you say?

Love: I was saying that I need to call Officer Byrd so I can tell him. Journey: Sure, call him, call him now.

Love (dialing): Yes, is Officer Byrd or Andrews in? Yes, I'll wait. (humming) Oh, hi, Officer Byrd, this is Love and I was wondering could you come over because I received a call. Okay, see you soon. He's coming over.

Journey: It's kind of odd to receive a call the second time and there is no number.

Love: It's Faith! I know it! Yet I can't see her father being in Florida, and if he is, what for! I mean why would he take our daughter over there? (crying) She was perfectly okay here in her school, huh.

Journey: Listen, it's 7:00 p.m. and it's been a long day. When Officer Byrd gets done, you need to go to bed. It will be all right, and in the end I pray you have her living with you. Honesty, dear, I see you are finished eating, but sit here until we get done with all this.

Officer Byrd: (Knocking)

Love: Hi, Offer Byrd. Come in, how are you this evening?

Officer Byrd: Well, I'm doing fine considering I'm working late. And you, ladies?

Love: We're tired too, but I called you because I received a phone call. I couldn't hear who it was, so that made me suspicious. I went and look at the machine, and the area showed Florida, but no number.

Officer Byrd: I see. Well, let me take this information back and run his name and have them check schools to see if Faith's name shows up.

Love: Oh, that would be wonderful! Officer Byrd: I'll be in touch. Bye now. (Both ladies say bye)

Journey: It will be okay. She's with her dad, and not a stranger. And they will find him.

Love: Now I see, there was a reason for you coming here. I couldn't get through this by myself; it's hard to live alone when you are going through a tragedy.

Journey: I know I lived in a shelter and if it wasn't for them me and Honesty would be in big trouble. So I know having someone there is a big help.

Love: I'm going to go lay down, I'm pooped. See you in the morning. Journey: Okay, and I'll say a prayer.

Love: Thanks for everything.

I took Honesty's hand and we went upstairs. I looked for her an outfit for the next day. While I was looking for her something to wear, she grabbed a note pad and started to write. I looked at what she was writing and she wrote, "Mercy and Hope are bad." I stood puzzled, I didn't know what she meant. This was too far-fetched for me. So I told Honesty to lie down, and that she needed to rest. I felt she had too much going on in her head. Getting her to rest I felt was the key to her healing. So she lay down and I did too.

At 1:00 a.m., Honesty was walking in her sleep, mumbling.

I woke up because I heard Honesty saying something. When I looked up, she was walking around, I told her to go back to bed.

Honesty pacing back and forth: No! Mercy! No, Hope!

I got up to try and calm her down. "Honey, quiet down before you wake Love. Honesty, dear, please come lie down. You need your rest. What is going on with you?

Honesty: Mercy, Hope, bad! Bad!

Journey: Please dear, you must keep your voice down. Okay, they both are bad I got it. But what can we do about it? I think she is a nice girl. So until we see differently, let's not worry, okay.

It's almost 2:00 a.m., so try to lay down, and we will talk about this later. So we went back to bed. I knew Honesty felt or saw something, but I just can't pinpoint it, and I still don't know why she drew Love's sister picture.

(At 7:00 a.m.)

Journey: I'm so tired this morning, and I got to go to work. Huh, Honesty dear, it's time to get up.

Honesty shook her head no.

Journey: I knew she was tired, but I couldn't stay home. Love: Journey! Are you up?

Journey: (yelling) Yes! Be down, I'm going to shower.

Love: Okay! (An hour later)

Love: Morning, how did you sleep?

Journey: Not good. Honesty was up at 1:00 a.m., and I told her she had to get up; but she is refusing, huh.

Love: Well, how about you take the car and I wait here until she wakes up. Then she and I can come then.

Journey: (stuttering) Well-well, I don't know. I mean she needs to be guided to the tub, she is starting to put on her own clothes but she can't see to comb her hair.

Love: I got it, I know she needs a lot of help and I will take care of it. Just go and open up the store. It's Saturday and it's your first day alone.

Journey: Oh, it is, isn't it? Okay, I will let her sleep, but let me go upstairs and lay her clothes out.

After I lay her clothes out, I went downstairs, grabbed me a bagel with cream cheese, a banana, and a cup of coffee and headed out.

Love: Drive safe. There are crazy people here in Bel-town! Bye. Journey: Bye.

Love: Well, I wonder what time Honesty will get up. I'll just make some pancakes with fresh blueberries and a few turkey patties. (Humming "I can see clearly now the rain is gone") Oh my, what was that thump I heard? Hmm, let me go see. Oh, my God! Honesty, are you okay? Umm, let me help you off the floor, sit here. Are you okay? You'll be all right, just relax. I know you can't see and it's hard to get around. Your mother had to go to work and she didn't want to wake you, so I told her to just go and I would help you get dressed and we would see her at work.

Since her clothes were laid out, they headed to the bathroom and ran her bath water. Then Honesty grabbed Love's hand and squeezed it hard.

Love: Honesty, you're hurting my hand. Wait! What are you doing? Why are you putting this pencil in my hand? No, dear, we don't have time and I can't draw anyway. Oh! You're squeezing my hand! Okay, I will try to draw, but I'm not good.

So Love turned off the water and went and sat on her chair. Honesty swiftly grabbed her hand, and really fast she drew the face of Mercy and Love's sister, Hope. She was shaking and shocked; and couldn't get words out.

Love: "How . . . did . . . you do . . . th-that? I can't draw; this is amazing. (laughing and excided) you helped me draw. (chuckles) Oh, Honesty honey, I got to call your mother. (dialing)

Journey: Faith's Gift Shop.

Love: (excited) Journey! You won't believe what Honesty just did.

THE SKETCHER

Journey: What did she do? Is she okay?

Love: Yes, silly. She's fine. I don't know how to explain this; I mean Honesty is a genius. I'll show you when we get there. (click)

Journey: (talking to self) I wonder what she is talking about. Oh my, I hope Honesty hasn't done something wild, I just feel something isn't right.

One hour later, Love comes through the door with a picture frame.

Love: Hi Journey! And hello, Lyric! Long time no see. Are you shopping for candles today? Well, take your time. We have new scented ones. Journey! Oh there you are. Hey, look at this picture.

Journey: OMG! What in the world!

Love: Didn't I tell you she has a gift? And you know what, she grabbed my hand and she helped me draw. Isn't that amazing! But what I don't understand is that she has never seen my sister. And why draw Mercy with my sister? How can she do that? I mean, draw people she has never seen. It's kind of spooky; she could have drawn a rose or an animal.

Journey: (stuttering) Well, she did see your sister. We saw her in your photo album. You said sister, right?

Love: Yes, my sister Hope. But Honesty can't see.

Journey: I-I know she can't see, but I described your sister to her. Excuse me, Honesty, come with me, dear. Honesty, what in the world are you doing? Why did you do that? You can't do this. Answer me! I know you can talk, speak and tell me why you did this? Oh God, help me to understand this gift. Honesty honey, listen. Doing what you did opened Love to your gift, and that isn't good. I found out that Hope is her sister; so how does she tie into this?

Love: (knocking) Can I come in?

Journey: Sure. Come in.

60

Love: Look, I'm sorry if I got Honesty in trouble. Journey: Oh no, she's not in trouble. She's a good girl.

Love: I know she is, but do you know that she could help people draw and you can make extra money?

Journey: I didn't know about that. I mean, I feel she would get tired with people coming to her and with her condition. I don't think it's a good idea.

Love: But we would control when they come for lessons. I can put up a sign advertising her gift; and that will be extra money in your pocket, not mine.

Journey: Well, when she wasn't blind it was okay for her to draw people; but now I don't know. I mean, I would have to tell her what they look like. And that would take up my time, but let me ask Honesty to see what she thinks.

Love: I don't understand when you say you have to describe what they look like. Did you tell her what Mercy looks like?

Journey: Umm, yes, I did.

Love: Oh, well, just ask her and see what she says. Hey, I think I'll hang this picture up so everyone can see what I did. I leave you two alone.

Journey: Honesty dear, I'm sorry I left this morning; but I had to be here at the store. Why don't you do some drawing while I help the customers? Give me a hug. Okay, just rest.

So I went out in front. It was so crowded, and Love was just taking it all in, and I started to.

Customer one: That is a beautiful picture up there. Who drew it?

Love: (proudly) I did.

Customer one: You! I didn't know you could draw. Can you draw me a picture of me and my husband together? You see, he has cancer, so it would be nice to have a picture of us just in case he pass away.

Love: Well . . . Journey: Sure, why not?

Love: Umm, sure. I can do it.

Customer one: How much for a big size? Love: Well . . .

Journey: I say $50.

Customer one: For that size! No, you can't be charging just fifty.

Love: Yes, and since you have been a valued customer, then that's my price to you.

Customer one: Well, thank you. When can I expect it to be ready?

Love: As soon as you bring me a picture, I can get right on it. By the way, what is your name, so I can write it down.

Customer one: Oh, sorry. It's Saniah, and I'll see you Monday. Bye. Journey: Oh no! What just happened?

Love: I don't know, and you haven't talked to Honesty yet, right?

Journey: No. But I felt sorry for that lady that's why I said why not.

I think I better go talk to Honesty, can you watch the floor for me?

Love: Sure, and I hope she says yes.

I headed to the back to have a little talk with Honesty. When I walked in, she had drawn a picture of the lady and her husband. I told her, no, no! She is not to do this here. So I took the picture and I hid it. I started to ask her how she knew what her husband looked like, but I caught myself because I knew about her gift. On the other hand, I never really knew what she was capable of doing.

Honesty wrote a note. "I drew that picture of Mercy and Hope together so when things come to pass, Love will see who her enemies are."

Journey: What? Don't stop. Tell me more. I know you can talk! What do you mean enemy? Honesty, I can't help you if you keep being quiet.

So I asked her would she be okay with helping Love draw so she and I could have extra money; she just shook her head no.

Love: How are things going back here? (Whispering) Is she okay with it?

Journey: Let's step out. No, she's not okay with it, and I hope I can continue working. You see, Honesty has become a handful and I don't know if . . . I'll be able to work.

Love: Don't worry, we can handle it. So, she said no?

Journey: Yes, she said no but I'll try later. Wow, 3:00 p.m. already and people been here all day.

Love: I love it! I invested in a great thing here. Excuse me. (Distant conversation) Hi, Passion! What brought you on this side of town?

Journey: Oh, well, I'll just sit behind the cash register. Hi, did you find what you are looking for?

Customer two: Yes, there are so many elegant things here. I got to bring my mother here. Umm, I was looking at that drawing of the two girls, and I was wondering, could the owner get in contact with the person who drew it? You see, my son is going to the marines and I would like to give him a drawing of me as a gift.

Journey: Well, the lady to talk to is right over there, and her name is Love.

Customer two: Love? Nice name. Oh thanks. Hello, my name is Nevaeh and I must say I love your store, but I was wondering about that painting you have hanging up, do you know who drew that?

Love: Yes! I did. But by the look on your face, I would say you're a little shocked. (chuckles)

Nevaeh: Well, yes. I never knew you, the owner, did art work.

Amazing.

Love: I do a little. So what did you have in mind?

Nevaeh: Like I was telling your helper, my son Saijae is going to the marines and I wanted to give him a sketch of me which would be a great gift.

Love: Oh how nice. So when do you want this done? Nevaeh: Is Tuesday okay? And where do we meet?

Love: Tuesday's fine, and we can meet here at the store. Just bring me a photo of you and that will be all I need.

Nevaeh: Oh, matter of fact I have one here in my purse. I just went and got them. See you Tuesday.

Love: Okay, I'll see you then and have a nice day. Oh gosh! Journey what have I done? I should have never put that drawing up there.

Journey: Yep, this is bad. Maybe you should take it down, and besides, Honesty hasn't agreed to help yet.

Love: But I like it, it's something I did.

Journey: Something you did? (chuckles) Look, it's clear Honesty helped you draw that picture, and you are getting and taking all the credit for it.

Love: Excuse me. I can't believe you said that; I did draw it.

Journey: No! Honesty helped you draw; and even if you still just wanted to give me the money, you are still getting the credit and not my daughter.

Love: You know, Journey, I thought I was doing you a favor by letting you work here, but I see I made a mistake. Maybe this job isn't for you, I don't think you are ready anyway.

Journey: Listen, Love, I didn't say that to make you mad. But it's true, Honesty helped you. Can you draw without her help?

Love was just silent. Journey: Well, can you?

Love: No, I can't! But it's how you said it to me. Journey: Love, I'm thankful you took me in and . . .

Love: Excuse me, my cell is ringing. Can you help that customer? Journey: Sure.

Love: Hello! Yes, Officer Andrews. Yes, oh you do? Sure, I'll be there. I got to go down to the police station. Officer Andrews think they have a lead, so if I don't come back just close.

Journey: Okay. Journey: Sure. Love: Thank you.

Journey: Huh, what a day.

I headed to the back to check on Honesty. When I walked in, she had drawn a picture of the lady whose son was going to the marines.

Journey: Honesty, no! no! I ask that you don't do this. Now we will have to take these pictures home and I will have to lie again and say I told you how they looked. Wait, but I don't know what the man looks like. Oh no! See where lying gets you. Let see, the lady is coming on Monday and the other on Tuesday. We just can't use them; we will have to wait until the one bring picture of her husband. Solved.

I looked at the clock and it was 5:00 p.m., so I locked up. Just as we were leaving, the women drove up with her husband photo. She told me she thought she should get the photo to us sooner; so I took it and we went home. When we got home, Love wasn't there yet, so we went in and I sat the pictures on the couch and Honesty and I sat down to rest.

Honesty started crying.

Journey: Honesty dear, what's wrong? Tell me, I can't keep guessing. Honesty continues to cry.

Journey: (hugging Honesty) It's okay, just let it out. I know everything has been going so fast and you are not well, but we will get through it. Let's go upstairs and get changed.

Door slams.

Love: Journey, I'm home! Wha-what's this? Wow, I see Honesty has been working without me. She drew these pictures for my customers.

Journey: Hey, you're back. How did it go?

Love: It wasn't him. They came across a man and a girl that kind of looked like them, but it wasn't.

Journey: What was the location?

Love: Florida. Umm … so when did she draw these?

Journey: Oh, I forgot to tell you that when she gets this feeling to draw she goes right at it.

Love: Did the one lady come back with picture?

Journey: Yep, and I'm glad she did. It's best to get it over with.

Love: Well, I don't understand how she can draw so fast. I still would like to know how she can do that. Does she have powers? Are you hiding something from me? I mean, I'm still shocked about what she did with my hand. I was so excited that I overlooked all of that. Tell me, what is going on with her.

Journey: I don't know! I mean things changed when she became blind. She is an artist as we know, so it's not strange or unusual.

Love: Yes, it is. But yet it's great! The women needed the pictures and

I decided to back up from trying to take the credit and let Honesty do it. I mean, it is her doing and I got a little crazy there, so sorry.

Journey: Apology accepted. Well, something has to come through for you and your daughter.

Love: I hope and pray. Oh, I will have Mercy to come get these pictures and take them to the ladies. I'm going to bed early. I ate a little while I was out.

Journey: Okay, good night.

So I went to the kitchen and made Honesty and me some soup and sandwiches. After a while, Honesty took out the picture she drew of the ocean and trees. She kept staring at it, and then she started walking back and forth holding her head. I called her name; she then stopped and just lay down and slept.

At 7:00 a.m.

Journey: Ugh, so early! I don't know if I should even get up. Oh it's Sunday. Oh gosh.

I got up anyway and made some coffee. Then Love came down. Love: Morning! And that coffee smells so good.

Journey: Did you sleep okay?

Love: No. I had a dream about Faith coming home, and it seemed so real. I just can't take this. I mean, why have he done this to me? I wonder, did it have something to do with child support? I bet he thought I was going to try and take Faith and drain him of all his money.

Journey: Child support? You think that's the reason? Well, don't overreact. Let the police work on this.

Then I heard Honesty screaming, so I ran upstairs and Love followed. When we got up there, Honesty had her hands over her ears and her nose was bleeding really bad.

Journey: Honesty! Honey, what's wrong? Love: I better call 911.

Journey: No! No! Don't call 911. It's pointless. I need to be alone with her.

Love: What! Don't call 911. Her nose is bleeding pretty bad. Journey: Trust me, it's pointless. Just leave me alone with her please.

Thank you.

(Door shuts) I asked Honesty to tell me what happened, but she said nothing and just put her head between her legs while she sat on the floor. Her nose was bleeding so bad that I had to get cold towels. While I was in the bathroom, she let out another scream. I ran out and then she said . . .

Honesty: Stop talking so loud! I can hear you! I'm right here. Journey: Honesty, who are you talking to?

Honesty: (in a small voice) I hear Faith talking about her mother to her dad, and she want to be with her mother. Stop it! You're hurting my ears. Make it stop, Mom!

Journey: Oh dear, this is something new going on with you. I would love to take you to the hospital, but I know there is nothing they can do.

So I just held her close to my chest, rocking her while holding the towel under her nose. Then she pulled away and sat up.

Honesty: She stopped.

Journey: (crying) Honesty, I'm sorry these strange things keep happening to you. If you can, can you tell me what you heard?

Honesty wrote it down on paper. "I heard Faith say to her dad that she wanted to see her mommy; and that she hates where they are and to take her home.

Journey: What is happening to you? This is new. You now can hear people talking even though they are far away. We know she is in Florida, but where? Listen, we can never tell Love what you can do. This should never get out. I feel bad that I know what Faith is saying and I can't even tell her mother but I will find away.

Phone rings.

Journey: Hello! Oh, hi, Love. Where are you? Yes, she's doing better. Why are you at the store on Sunday? Oh rearranging things. Okay, well,

I'm going to the shelter to go to Bible study. I think it will do Honesty some good. Okay, bye. Come on, Honesty, let's get you dressed.

At 10:00 a.m.

We arrived at the shelter and we heard singing, so we just walked in and sat down in the back row. Then after the singing was over, thepastor spoke.

Pastor: Glory to God, give him praise today. Well, it is a blessing to see you all here today, and it is a blessing to be alive. God has given us another day to get it right and to get closer to him. Today, I would like to study the letter to the Corinthians chapter twelve, which is about spiritual gifts. Let's start at verse four. As you can see from reading, this verse says that there are all kinds of gifts, but the same Spirit. And verse five says there are differences of ministries, but the same Lord. Then verse six says again that there are diversities of activities, but it is the same God who works all in all. What I would like to say is, all of you sitting here has a gift from God and you should use it. You may not want to but it is a gift, and when you decided to use that gift God gave you, then you will be blessed. Amen!

At noon

Maleaka: Journey and Honesty, nice to see you here. How are you?

Journey: We are fine, thanks to God. And I must say the pastor had a good message on gifts.

Maleaka: Yes, it was a good message. Honesty has a wonderful gift and it is from God. So are you on your way home?

Journey: Yes, got to get Honesty home. She gets tired fast but we will try and stop by again.

Maleaka: Okay. Well, nice seeing you. Bye, Honesty. On Monday 9:00 a.m. at the store.

Mercy: Hi, Journey. How did you do on Saturday?

Journey: I did fine. I was kind of nervous, but Love helped me out. It went well.

Mercy: Good. And look at Honesty looking pretty in her black dress. Nice. How are you, Honesty?

Journey: She's not feeling good. I'll just take her to the back office and let her rest.

Mercy: Oh, sorry to hear that. Okay, I'll be up front if you need me. Journey: Oh, where is Love? She left early this morning

Mercy: She had to make a run.

Journey: Okay.

So I went to the back to start my filing and to let Honesty rest. As I started to file, Mercy came in.

Mercy: There are ladies out here who want to see you.

Journey: Me? I got up and went out. There were the two ladies who wanted their pictures drawn. Journey: Well, hi. How are you?

Customer 1: Hi! I just stopped by to tell Love thanks for the picture she drew for me.

Customer 2: And I wanted to say thanks too. It's beautiful. Mercy:

I didn't know Love drew.

Journey: It's a long story. Love: I'm back!

Mercy: You mean to tell me those pictures I took to the ladies you drew? You didn't tell me you drew.

Love: Drew? Drew what!

Mercy: Those pictures I picked up from your house.

Love: Oh, those pictures. Ha, well, Honesty was teaching me how to draw, that's all.

Mercy: How is she teaching you? She is blind. And how did you learn so fast?

Love: Oh, I'm a fast learner. And her being blind and still can draw is a gift.

Mercy: Wow! Amazing! Journey, is this true that Honesty can teach people to draw?

Journey: Well, sort of. I mean, she doesn't do it on a regular basis. Mercy: Could she teach me?

Journey: I'm sure she could, but she's been going through a lot. She hasn't even been drawing for the public at all.

Mercy: Well, I hope she gets better so she can teach me. Okay, I better get back to work.

Journey: Oh my-my-my, what has happened here? Let me get busy. It's 11:00 a.m. Oh, Honesty dear, are you hungry?

Honesty just shook her head no.

Journey: Well, you didn't eat anything this morning. Here's an apple and a cereal bar. Here, take it. Thank you. Okay, now let's see. That goes there in that pile.

Then I heard something hit the floor. I looked around; Honesty had dropped the apple and bar on the floor. So I just took that as she didn't want it. Then she got up.

Journey: Honesty honey, you can't see, so be careful. Touch the wall as you go.

She then went out and I kept working.

Honesty walked upon Mercy talking on her cell phone.

Mercy's conversation: Oh, thank you, Kavarri, for letting me take a vacation in that beautiful home of yours. I felt kind of bad that I lied to Love about working at another job. But my girlfriends loved it too. Hey, how is Faith? How could she not love it in Lauderdale Lakes? So have you talked with your sister-in-law, Hope? Oh, she's coming there, nice. Does Faith know she's coming? Oh good. Well, I got to go before someone catches me. Yes, I will be there too. I want to see what it looks like there. Okay, bye.

Honesty feels her way back to the office and just flops down in the chair, shaking her head.

Journey: What is it, Honesty? Why are you acting like this, what is wrong?

Honesty: (whispers) Mercy, Kavarri, and Hope are bad. Journey: What happened?

Then she got her pen and wrote Mercy, Hope and Kavarri's name and the town.

Journey: Honesty what do this mean? Do you think they are hiding something from Love? I got to figure this out. How to tell her Faith is in Lauderdale Lakes and that Kavarri and Hope know something? This is so hard, Honesty. Can you help me? God, I know where she is and I can't say. I will come up with something. It's going on 1:00 p.m. and I got to get this filing done. Honesty dear, just relax.

Love: Hey, girls! How are things going back here? Journey: Oh, slow but I'm getting there.

Love: Well, when we are done here we can go out to eat

Journey: That sounds good. Umm, Love, why doesn't your sister ever call you?

Love: She's strange like that. She's caught up into money and vacations.

Journey: Really? You said she doesn't even know that Faith is gone, right?

Love: Nope. And I'd rather keep it that way.

Journey: I see. Okay, dinner after work sounds good. Huh, what a day. I don't know if I can work any further. I'm drained. Honesty, it's getting close to 2:00 p.m., just relax. You haven't eaten all day, how can you do that? I don't understand what has happened with your appetite.

Honesty starts to cry.

Journey: Honesty dear, what is wrong? Oh, I can't get any work done. Why are you crying? Love! Love! Can you come back here please?

Love: Yes, what's wrong? Why is Honesty crying?

Journey: I don't know why she is crying and I don't see how I'm going to work with Honesty like this.

Love: Look, we were all going to go eat after work, but I think you need to go home now.

Journey: Are you sure?

Love: Yes, go, go. I'll be fine. Journey: Okay, I see you at the house.

I got Honesty and her drawings and headed home. When we got there, I took her upstairs and ran her some bath water so she could relax. I sat down by the tub and I asked her why she was crying.

Honesty said in a soft voice: I was crying because Faith wants to come home to her mother.

The whole time she was talking, her eyes were closed. But when she laid backed in the tub and opened her eyes, it scared me because they turned all black. I never knew how black her eyes were up close. I hated what has happen to my daughter. I don't know if it's a gift or a curse. I believe in God and I also know he has a purpose for all of us, but I pray he heals her.

Journey: Honesty, it's time to get out and dry off. Here is your pj's now get into bed.

She pointed to her painting. I told her she could draw, but just for a little while. I took a shower. When I got out and saw it was 5:00 p.m. already, I went downstairs. A thought came to me that I should call Officer Byrd or Andrews and try to say something, but I didn't want toget involved. I picked up the phone anyway.

Journey: Hello! Is Officer Andrews or Byrd in? Yes, I can wait. Hi, Officer Byrd. This is Journey, Love's friend. Yeah. Well, I was thinking, have you ever thought of checking other areas in Miami.

Officer Byrd: I have, but nothing. But we won't give up. Journey: Have you heard of Lauderdale Lakes?

Officer Byrd: Yes, why you ask?

Journey: Well, I heard Love talking about how her husband loved it when they would vacation there. So that might be a place to check. But if you could, could you not tell her I told you? I don't want her to think I'm getting in her business.

Officer Byrd: Sure thing. You're just a concerned friend. Bye now.

Journey: Okay, bye. It worked. Oh, my God it worked! Okay, now let me cook something. I'm starved. Honesty! Come down and be careful while coming down the stairs. Honesty it worked, Officer Byrd is going to check Lauderdale Lakes. I had to lie, and you know I hate lying, but no one can know what you can do. Everything is going to be all right and you will soon have a friend to talk to when Faith comes home. I got done with cooking; here's a turkey burger and chips and a glass of milk. It's kind of nice sitting here in this big house. I mean, we haven't had a home in a while and I know that you could with your drawing make us enough money to live nice, but you can't now. Are you done already? You didn't eat that much, dear. You want to lie down and listen to the TV? Okay, I'll take you to the living room. Now I can go eat then clean the kitchen.

As I started to wash the dishes, the phone rang. It was Love. Journey: Hey, Love! Oh, she's fine. How's your dinner going? Nice.

I'm sure Mercy is enjoying being out. Oh, okay, we will be here.

So I hung up the phone and finished cleaning the kitchen. Then the phone rang again.

Journey: Oh, hi Officer Byrd. No, Love isn't here. Is something wrong?

Officer Byrd: Well, I must say, if it wasn't for you we wouldn't have caught him.

Journey: Caught him did you say? Are you serious!

Officer Byrd: Yep, and he is in custody, and Faith is with child protective services. So have Love to call me.

Journey: Love has her cell; you can call her on it. Officer Byrd: Okay, thanks. Bye.

Journey: Honesty! Honesty! Did you hear me? Well, that was Officer Byrd and they found Faith. Isn't that wonderful?

Honesty speaking in a low tone: Now Love will come face to face with her enemies.

Journey: You're right dear, Love has to fly to Miami. And if I'm right, Love won't tell Mercy or her sister Hope because she don't want them to know that Faith is even gone, yet they do know and they will all meet there and the truth will come out.

Honesty went silent. Phone rings

Journey: (anxiously speaking) Hello! Love, is this you? Yes, Officer Byrd called and he told me the good news. Okay, I'll see you when you get home, bye. Honesty dear, I think you better lie down, it's been a long day for you.

So while Honesty lie down I sat back and thought if I should keep working. It's so hard with my daughter being sick and all; and I see her gift wears her out. I needed to talk to Love about this again.

Door opens

Love: Journey! I'm home.

Journey: I know you are happy this is all over. Go ahead and cry.

Love: Yes! Yes! I'm glad it's over and I got to fly there tomorrow to get my baby girl.

Love: I can't wait to see my Faith, and when she comes we all will have some fun. Honesty and her aren't that far apart in age. Hey, did you tell me you were saying prayers for me?

Journey: Yes, I did.

Love: Well, I see it works. I got to start doing that more often. Well, I'm going to my room to change and pack.

Journey: Okay, get some rest. Say, Love, never mind. We'll talk later. (talking to herself) I will tell her I will not able to work but I will let her get past all that's going on first. Well, it's bed time.

On Tuesday morning at 7:00 a.m. in the kitchen.

Journey: I'll make some coffee. (humming "It's a beautiful morning") Love: Morning! Today's the day I get to see my Faith.

Journey: I'm so happy this is over for you.

Honesty standing at top of stairs: Mother! Please come.

Journey: Be there, dear. Love, what time does your plane leave? Love, at 8:40 a.m.: Hey! Honesty just spoke. Wow!

Honesty: Mother, come here!

Journey: Let me see what Honesty wants, and I would like to speak with you before you leave.

So I went upstairs, and Honesty took me by the hand into the room and she whispered.

Honesty: Did you tell Love that her sister and Mercy will be there? Journey: No, honey. I wouldn't do that, but let me go say bye to Love.

I thought to myself, wow, this is going to be a mess. None of them knew that they are going to run into each other there.

Love: Journey, I'm going to go. (phone rings) Hello! Oh, hi, Mercy! Yes, oh you can't make it to work. Oh, you're not feeling good. Well, Journey is here. She can come in for you. Okay, bye.

Journey: I heard, and yes, I will go open up the store. Love: And can you be there on time?

Journey: I'll be there on time. Have a safe trip. Bye. (door slams) When she gets there she'll be in for a rude awakening. Mercy just lied. But I'm no better. Oh, well, let me get Honesty and myself dressed.

I headed upstairs, and when I got there, Honesty was dressed. I was in shock because she couldn't see.

Journey: Honesty dear, you got dressed on your own.

Honesty, speaking in a low voice: I can do it now. You have done enough for me.

Journey, with tears in her eyes: Oh, Honesty I don't mind. I mean, you are my daughter and I love you. I'm going to get dressed and then we can go.

So I got dressed. I wasn't really up to it but someone had to run the store. When we arrived at the store, as usual, people were lined up to get in. So I opened the door and the people just flooded the place.

Journey: Honesty, you sit over there and do some drawing. When noon comes we can eat.

In Florida

Love (talking to herself: I'm here! Okay, I need a taxi to the jail. Wow, it's nice here, great! There's a whole line of taxis. Hi, can you take me to the county jail?

At Florida's jail

Love: Thank you. Hi, my name is Love Robinson and I'm here to see Officer Wesson.

Receptionist: Have a seat please.

Officer Wesson: Hello, you must be Love. Love: Correct.

Officer Wesson: Follow me, Mrs. Robinson. I need you to pick your ex-husband out in a line up, just so we know we have the right man. (speaking through speaker) Send them out!

Love: No, not him, not him, no, no, yes! Yes! That's my ex.

Officer Wesson: And may I say that just in case you wanted to know, no, he couldn't see you.

Love: May I ask where is my daughter?

Officer Wesson: She's on the other side. I will have them to bring her to you. (calling) Yes, this is officer Wesson, can you bring Faith Robinson over here to me. What do you mean? Oh, her aunt and a friend came and got her? Who allowed this? Oh, the father gave the okay for her to be released to them. Then where are they?

Love: What's going on?

Officer Wesson: I was told that the auntie and a friend came here to pick her up.

Love: Who, my sister? We don't even talk. She knows nothing about this, and what friend?

Officer Wesson: I'll take you to them. Love, talking to herself:

Who are these pretenders? Maybe it's his girlfriend.

Officer Wesson opens the door. Faith: Mom! (Hugging her)

Love looks over and there sits Mercy and Hope.

Love: OMG! Hope! Mercy! What is going on? Why are you two here? And Mercy, you told me you were sick and that's why you couldn't work today, you liar!

Officer Wesson: Calm down, Mrs. Robinson. Let me ask the questions. So, Hope, who are you?

Hope: I'm Love's sister.

Officer Wesson: And who might you be?

Mercy: I'm Mercy and I'm a friend of Mr. and Mrs. Robinson and an employee of hers.

Officer Wesson: Tell me, how do you two play a part in this?

Love: I'm in shock. Why Mercy and why Hope? How can you both know what he did yet not tell me! Mercy, you are fired, and Hope we never did talk and we can continue not talking.

Mercy: I'm sorry, I just didn't want to hurt you but I guess I did. I need a job! I got bills!

Hope: I'm sorry. But like you said, we don't talk, so I felt why call you about this.

Love: Sorry won't cut it! Come on, Faith.

Officer Wesson: Well, ladies, I have to book you since you are involved. I thought you were here to just pick Faith up, but there's more to this story.

Hope: Book! Why? I can't have anything on my record. I work for a university.

Officer Wesson: Well, that's the law. So both of you follow me. Mercy: I can't have this on my record either; where will I work? Officer Wesson: Yeah, and I can't retire right now. Mrs. Robinson, you can go. But I'm afraid Hope and Mercy may face charges; accessory to the crime is big.

Love: And they should. Let's go home, dear, and I don't want to see Kavarri.

Faith: Mom, it's nice to be back with you and far as dad. I don't know what he was thinking, I told him I didn't want to go.

Love: I know, dear. But your dad just wants to control everything, he was always running things in his line of work and that spilled over into our marriage.

Faith: It's sad to say, but I don't feel sorry for him, Mercy, nor Auntie Hope.

Love: Just so you will know, we have two guests who are great people. But the girl, there is something wrong with her. She does strange things that I don't understand.

At the Florida airport

Love: Thanks for the ride. Let's get in line. Hi, I need one ticket to Seattle, Washington.

Faith: Mom, since Mercy doesn't work for you anymore, can I help you in the store?

Love: Sure, dear. I opened the shop with you in mind. Yes, got your ticket. Let's see what time our plane leaves. Okay, it leaves at 4:00 p.m. which is in one hour. Are you hungry?

Faith: A little. Dad did feed me. It was all healthy food.

Love: He did well on that, you know. This is a nice airport. Oh, there's a restaurant over there, let's go in.

Faith: You see places like this in Florida all the time, Mom; they are so nice.

Love: Oh, you're a tourist now? Ha! Waitress: May I take your order?

Love: Yes, I would like a green tea with your homemade soup. Waitress: And you, little lady?

Faith: I would like an ice tea with a bagel and cream cheese. Waitress: Okay, coming up.

Love: Faith, I can't believe you are sitting here with me. I panicked when I found out you were gone. I told the police, and they kept looking and they found you.

Faith: I tried to call but it wouldn't go through. Love: I was told someone called, but it was static.

Faith: Yeah, I was in a bad area.

Waitress: Okay, here's your soup and green tea, and here's your bagel and cream cheese and ice tea. Anything else?

Love: No, that's it, thanks. Well, let's eat. Time goes by so fast.

Yummy, this soup is great.

Faith: Mom, can I start right away working at the store?

Love: Yes, you can, and I can't wait for you to meet Honesty. I guess I need to let you know about her a little bit more. She is blind but she wasn't born blind. The blindness happened to her over night. It's pretty weird how she does things.

Faith: Really, she sounds scary.

Love: Don't' be scared. Just look at her as if she were normal. Faith: I'll try.

Love: Okay, we are done and we got to go. Let's pay up front. Okay, thank you and the food was great. Come on, Faith, they are lining up.

Back at Florida's jail

Mercy: I can't believe I'm in jail. I mean, I didn't do anything, but didn't tell Love.

Hope: Well, what did I do? But the same, I'm scared. Mercy: Me too, but they have guards so.

Officer Wesson: Well, ladies, it looks like you and Mr. Robinson will have to spend time in jail until Monday. Then you go in front of a judge, unless you bail out; but you will have to come back to court.

Mercy, crying: I'm too young for this. I can't believe this is happening to me.

Officer Wesson: Do you want to make a phone call?

Mercy: No, I don't want my family to know. Well, I can call and make up something.

Officer Wesson: Okay, over there is the phone and you get one phone call.

Hope: I guess I'll call my husband to tell him what has happened.

I'm sure he's been calling my cell but it's locked up.

Mercy (dialing, phone ringing): Hello, Mom, how are you? That's good. I'm calling because I'm out of town with friends and I will call you when I get back. Okay, tell dad I love him. Bye. (Crying) I can't lie to my parents.

Hope: We can bail out like he said. Maybe my brother-in-law can bail us out since he got us into this mess. But first let me call my husband, Denali.

Mercy: Does he know?

Hope: Umm, a little. But I will have to explain now that I'm here. (dialing, phone ringing) Hi honey! Where am I? Well, I'm in Florida, in jail. Honey, calm down. I know this is a shock, but you sort of knew because I told you a little about what was going on with my ex brother-in-law and his daughter. No! I don't need you down here but I may have to bail out and I'm going to see if Kavarri can bail me and Mercy out. Anyway, just stay by the phone. Love you, bye.

Mercy: Oh, God! Why me, I shouldn't have gotten involved.

Hope: Don't beat yourself up over this. You are a friend to him and friends get into a lot of trouble sometimes for one another. Officer! Officer!

Officer: Yes.

Hope: Umm, is there a way to get a message to Kavarri Robinson to bail us out?

Officer: Yes, there is. I'll be right back.

Mercy: Your sister fired me and I needed the money to start my own business. Now I don't know what I'm going to do.

Hope: Don't worry. You'll find a job. You got a degree.

Mercy: Are you forgetting that we are in here due to accessory to a crime?

Hope: No, I'm not forgetting. Oh come on, officer, where is he? Officer: Okay, ladies, you both have been bailed out.

Mercy: But we will still have to go to court, like fly back here. I don't have money to do that.

Hope: Don't worry, Kavarri will have to take care of you since he got you into this.

Officer: Well, ladies, you can go. Mr. Robinson took care of you and you can meet him downstairs. Make sure you stop by property.

Hope: Okay, bye. Let's get the heck out of here. Where is this property window?

Mercy: Over there.

Hope: Hi, I'm Hope Humphrey and I'm here to pick up my property. Property lady: Here you go, and who are you?

Mercy: I'm Mercy Henderson. Thank you.

Hope: Now let's find Kavarri. There's the stairs, there he is, Kavarri!

Kavarri: Hey, before you two say anything, I'm sorry for even involving you and I will try my hardest to get you two out of this. Let's get a taxi to the airport, we will take the next flight.

Mercy: What about your car and clothes? Kavarri: I'll get it all shipped.

Arriving at Florida's airport

Mercy: Where are you going to live?

Kavarri: In my house where you stayed that night with your girls. Mercy: I've been staying there, and how is that going to look?

Kavarri: Right, well, can't you live with your parents for a while until all of this is over? Then I will get you a place, but you will have to pay your own bills.

Mercy: Fair enough.

Hope: Are you going to pay my bills, ha.

Kavarri: Funny, Hope. You work at a university. You and your husband are professors and I think you have enough money.

Hope: Yeah, we do but you do too. Kavarri: Let's get in line.

Hope: Your ex-wife my sister is very upset with us.

Kavarri: Look, Hope, you know why I left with my daughter. I just wanted to start a new life after the divorce. And since I had custody, I didn't see anything wrong in leaving. Yeah, I was to tell her but you know she would have stopped me.

Hope: Yeah, I know you just wanted to get away but now look.

Kavarri: I was going to let her know after I got settled. She didn't have to panic; and besides, Faith was okay with it. She was having fun with her new friends who after they graduated would go to Harvard. She and her friends are 4.0 and have maintained it the whole school year.

Hope: So she didn't really miss, Love?

Kavarri: Yes, she missed her mother, but she's a teen and they love life. I had her involved in all types of activities.

Hope: Did she try to call Love?

Kavarri: Not as I know of, I mean it would have showed up on the phone bill.

Hope: I hate waiting. Come on.

Kavarri: Hi, can you tell me when is your next flight to Seattle and Anaheim, California?

Ticket lady: 5 minutes they will be boarding for Anaheim California and for Seattle one hour from now.

Hope: Yes! 5 minutes.

Kavarri: Okay, give me three tickets.

Hope: Thanks, Kavarri, for buying my ticket.

Kavarri: It's the least I can do, I got you two into this and I got to get you out. What we all will do is wait for a letter that will give us a court date and we all will fly back here, and hope the judge won't give us jail time.

Hope: I'd rather do community service. Mercy: Me too. Actually not.

Lady speaks over the intercom: We are now boarding at Gate One for Anaheim California.

Kavarri: Okay, call me when you make it home, and you are a wonderful sister-in-law.

Hope: Yeah–yeah, will do. An hour later

Kavarri: Let's make it, Mercy.

Voice of Journey: So they got on the plane. But Little did any of us know that we all would be in for the shock of our life.

Arriving in Seattle

Mercy: We are finally here, and I'm here with no job.

Kavarri: Don't worry. I'll get you a job. You know I know people I could have gotten you a job before but you wanted to work in a gift shop.

Mercy: Well, a woman loves gifts, right?

Kavarri: You got that right. I'll call you at your mom's. I got business to take care of.

Mercy: Okay, thanks. Back at gift shop

Journey: Well, it's almost time to close and I haven't heard anything from Love. (Cell rings) Oh, this might be her. Hello, hey Love! How did it go? Oh great, you got her. Okay, I'll see you at home. Bye. Well, Honesty, that was Love and she got Faith with her. Isn't that wonderful? The store is clearing out so let's lock up and head home.

So we went home. When we arrived, Love was there checking the mail.

Love: Hey, Journey and Honesty! How was it at the store?

Journey: It went well. How was your trip?

Love: It was fast and I had a little surprise when I got there, let's go in.

So we went in and Honesty went upstairs. Journey: Be careful going up, dear. Where's Faith?

Love smiling: Oh she's upstairs settling in. It is so great to have her home. But before you meet her, let me tell you who was there when I got there.

Upstairs, Honesty hears music playing as she passes by Faith's room door.

Back downstairs

Journey: I can't believe what you just told me. Your sister and Mercy were there and you fired Mercy.

Love: I didn't want to, but I had no choice, Journey. What would you have done? And my sister, how could she do this to me?

Journey: OMG! This is terrible.

Love: Well, like I said, there's no bad reason why we had stopped talking. It was just she thought she and her husband were better than I and Kavarri. So we just backed away, that was it.

Journey: That's the reason, wow.

Love: Oh, well, life goes on. Come, meet Faith. Journey: Okay.

Love, walking upstairs: Faith! Faith! (she pushes door open) Faith, this is Journey.

Both say hi

Journey: Oh, Love, she is beautiful. Where did she get those green eyes?

Love: It comes from her dad's side, and her dad is handsome. So there you have it. Faith is going to be helping me in the shop since Mercy isn't there.

Journey: That's great! Help is needed for sure now. Come on, Faith, and meet Honesty.

When I walked in, Honesty was drawing. Journey: Honesty, I want you to meet someone. She stood up but her head was down.

Love: Faith, this is Honesty, and Honesty this is faith. Faith: Hi! Glad to meet you.

Journey: (Honesty remained silent) Honesty dear, this is Faith. She is home now and you two can be friends.

Love: We will leave you and Honesty alone. Journey: Okay.

Love: Come help me cook dinner, Faith. Faith: You cook now?

Love: (chuckles) No, but I try.

Faith: Mom, what happened to Honesty's eyes? I mean, she's pretty, but her eyes scare me. And does she wear shades to cover up her eyes?

Love: Yes, she wears shades. I knew you would ask me this, but I don't know why or how it all happened. The doctors don't even know why, but I'm sure they are doing some research. She is very sweet. Maybe you two can get together and talk. She goes to the shop with Journey. It's good for her to get out.

Faith: Why? That's not a good place for her to be, everyone will see her.

Love: Faith, she's fine. She can't stay in the house. Faith: Well, I don't want to work there; she scares me.

Love: Oh, Faith, stop it. She's okay. She sits in the back office. It will be fine, come on help me cook.

Faith: Okay.

Journey: Honesty dear, why didn't you say hi to Faith? You should feel close to her since you knew what was going on with her. I think you two should start hanging out, you need a friend.

Honesty in a low voice: I'm fine, I don't need friends.

Journey: Why you don't need friends? We all need friends, just because you are blind doesn't mean you stay to yourself. I got a good idea, how to break the ice between you and Faith. Draw a picture of her in Florida, and she will be amazed that you can do that. Okay, do it for me.

Honesty in a low voice: Okay, Mom, for you.

Journey: That's my girl. Let's go downstairs, I smell dinner. Love: Well, with help I'm cooking! Ha!

Journey: Good. Now I can taste your cooking, or more or less Faith's cooking ha. So what's cooking?

Love: Well, Faith and I roasted some potatoes, fried cabbage and steak on the grill.

Journey: Sounds good, can't wait to eat. Umm, Love, I need to speak with you in private.

Love: Sure, Faith, why don't you and Honesty go in the TV room and get to know each other, then we will eat.

Journey: Well, I know this may come as a shock to you, but I can't continue to work at the shop with Honesty's condition. The getting up early and dragging her out is a bit too much for her.

Love: I see. I got Faith here to help me, and if I need to I can always hire someone. It's okay, I will make it. Just thought you needed the cash.

Journey: I do need the money, but it's hard right now. I don't want to lay up on you either, so I can do the cooking and cleaning and that can be my job.

Love: Oh yeah, not a bad idea. Okay. (house phone rings) Excuse me. Hello! Why are you calling here? You are supposed to go through your lawyer. No! You can't talk to her. Faith has been through enough mess, so why would you want to get her upset?

Kavarri on the phone: She is my daughter! Now let me talk to her. Love: (click)

Journey: Are you okay?

Love: Yes, it's just that I know he won't stop until he gets her back. But if he goes to jail, I won't have to worry about it.

Journey: Do you really want him to go to jail? I mean, I don't think Faith would be so happy about that.

Love: Don't try and make me feel like the bad guy here. You have seen all I've been through, so you tell me should I care what happens to him.

Journey: Yes, you should. If Faith even sees you acting like this, what message will you be sending to her?

Love: Faith is the one who said they all deserve what they get. Let me deal with this. (sarcastically she said) Thanks for your concern.

Journey: Yeah anytime. Love: Girls! Let's eat.

Faith: Smells good, Mom. Love: Thanks to you, my dear.

Faith: Umm, Mom, what's for dessert?

Love: Ha, you thought I forgot, well it's a surprise. Faith: Come on, Mom, what is it?

Love: No, I'm not saying. Just eat and after dinner you will see. Journey: Honesty, let me fix your plate.

Love: Journey, Honesty is pretty smart. Let her try at least.

Journey: I don't think she should be doing this, and I wouldn't want her to waste food on your nice table cloth.

Love: My word, I'm not worried about this table cloth There is such thing as dry clean.

Journey: We can avoid that. Here's your plate, Honesty. So, Faith, tell me, what kind of things you like to do for fun?

Faith: Oh, I like to play golf, swim, and run track.

Journey: Nice. Well, Honesty likes to draw and draw. They all laughed except Honesty.

Love: Okay, I'll bring out the dessert. Here it is, red velvet cake!

Faith: Yummy, Mom, my favorite!

Journey: I love red velvet cake. My mother used to make it.

Love: Where is your mother and father? You never talk about them.

Journey: No, I don't because it's sad that my parents didn't get to meet Honesty.

Love: Girls, why don't you go in the other dining room and eat your cake.

Faith: Sure, let's go, Honesty.

Journey: Thanks for doing that. I don't like to talk about her grandparents in front of her.

Love: So what happened to them?

Journey: Well, when I was about ten years old, my father died in a house fire. After the police investigated, they found out it was the wrong house these boys set on fire. It was suppose to have been two houses down from my parents' home. Some type of initiation.

Love: Oh my God!

Journey: Yes, these boys were paid to do it. My mother is still alive but she lives in Hawaii.

Love: Hawaii! What is she doing there?

Journey: Well, after the death of my father, my mother sent me to live with my grandparents in Portland Oregon while she healed from what had happened. In the meantime, she met a lawyer from Hawaii. They ended up getting married and she moved there with him. Thank God for my grandparents, they both worked for the government. They took care of me well. later I met my ex-husband Jeremiah. We dated for six years then we got married. Then I had Honesty. I sent my mother pictures of Honesty, but that's all she saw of her.

Love: So your mother is still alive but never met Honesty?

Journey: Yep, I don't know why she's being this way. Maybe her husband has some control issues. I haven't had the money to go see her. I do want her to see her granddaughter.

Love: Well, maybe we'll all take a trip there Journey: That would be great!

Upstairs

Faith: You have really long hair and it's soft to brush. Tell me, how come you are not in school?

Honesty says in a low voice: I don't know.

Faith: It would be fun to get out and meet friends. Maybe you should ask your mom. Could you sign up?

Honesty shakes her head no.

Faith: Sorry. Well, your hair is brushed. Hey, why is there a picture of Florida? Have you been there? Wow! You are a great artist. Hey, maybe your mother will let you go with me to a friend's birthday party. I'll ask her and this boy who likes me is going to be there too. He has been waiting for me. (chuckles)

Honesty whispers: Is he telling the truth? Faith: I think he is, why you ask?

Honesty responded not.

Journey, yelling from downstairs: Honesty! Dear, it's getting close for you to rest.

Faith: Let me go downstairs and tell her. Umm, Journey, my friend's birthday party is tomorrow. Is it okay if Honesty go? I will keep an eye on her.

Journey: I don't see why not. She needs to get out. Sure, she can go. Faith: Good. We will have fun. Okay, I'll go tell my mother.

Journey walks upstairs: Honesty dear, do you want to go with Faith to the birthday party?

Honesty was silent. Journey: Is that a no? Honesty whispers: I'll go.

Journey: It will be fun. So get some rest.

Next morning at 6:00 a.m., Love's cell phone rings.

Love: Love: Hello! Oh hi to the best lawyer in town. What's new? Oh, so Kavarri, my sister, and Mercy may get probation? Really, and he will pay me child support? Okay, we will stay in touch. Bye. (cell rings again) Hello, Kavarri! What are you doing calling me. I can't help that, my lawyer sent you a letter. What! You should want to pay child support. Oh, I don't want to hear anything from you after you took Faith away. Oh, go dig yourself a hole and stay there. I don't care! What do you want? If you don't stop calling, I will get a restraining order now. Bye. Huh. This man. Let me get up for work.

Faith: Morning, Mom.

Love: Oh, hi honey. Why you up so early?

Faith: Well, I'm excited about working, and you yelling at dad woke me up. Why can't you two get along?

Love: Oh, so your tune has changed? Well, we would if he wouldn't try and be so slick. He got everyone involved like your auntie and Mercy who worked for me. They all hid everything from me, Faith, and that was not right.

Faith: I know, Mom, but I was okay, and you two should get along for my sake. And are they going to jail?

Love: They may, they committed a crime.

Faith: Can't you drop the charges? I mean, it is dad and your sister.

Love: Honey, you are asking me to let them get away with the crime they committed. They need to learn a lesson.

Faith: Mom, is it worth it? I mean I'm sure the judge can find another punishment.

Love: I don't know. Let me think about this. Get dressed and eat breakfast so we can go. And you are going back to your school tomorrow morning. You can't be out like this.

Faith: I know, Mom. I love school and I know you are just letting me rest because of what I've been through.

Journey: Morning everyone! Love: Morning! How's Honesty?

Journey: She's fine and looking forward to going with Faith later today. I hope they have fun. How are you?

Love: Umm, Kavarri called this morning mad because he has to pay child support and he's upset because he can't talk to Faith. Right now, he needs to wait until all of us are relaxed and calm before he start calling.

Journey: I know it's hard, but you act like you still have feelings for him.

Love: I would have stayed with him if he wasn't so greedy. I mean he has good about him but the money went to his head. Anyway I got to focus on today.

Journey: You and Faith just go and have a great day, and Honesty will be ready to go later to the birthday party.

Love: Thanks, I will try. Come on, Faith, let's go. Bye, see you later.

Journey: Okay, bye. Honesty dear, what are we going to do today? Why don't we go surprise Jania.

Back at Mercy's parents' house

Mercy, calling Kavarri: Hello, Kavarri! Are you at home? Kavarri: No, I'm at the shop waiting for Love to get here.

Mercy: Are you crazy! You shouldn't be there, this could cause more problems.

Kavarri: I don't care, I must see Faith. She's my daughter and Love can't stop me from seeing her.

Mercy: I hope and pray this goes well. We will talk later, bye. Love: Okay, dear, we made it to work and this is your first day. Faith: I got a job. Yahoo!

Love: Let's go through the backdoor. Kavarri! What are you doing here?

Faith: Dad! How are you, and you look nice in your suit.

Kavarri: Thanks, dear. Love! Don't call the police. I just want to see Faith, that is all.

Love: I know you do, but did you care about my feelings when you took her away from me without telling me? You were wrong for that and you expect me to be nice to you. Okay, you've seen her, now go!

Kavarri: You are evil, Love, and you will get a call from my lawyer.

Love: And you will get a call from mine. Faith, go inside the shop. Faith: Mom, why can't you and dad just get along?

Love: Honey, it's not that we don't want to get along. It's just we are both angry and sometimes it takes a lawyer to clear things up. Okay, sweet heart?

Faith: Okay. So where do you want me to start?

Love: Well, you can get behind the counter, and I will go do some filing.

Journey at Jania's house Knock, knock

Door opens

Jania: OMG! Journey! Honesty! Come in, how are you two doing?

Journey: Well, we are doing fine, and you?

Jania taking a deep breath: Well, I'm alone now and I thought I told you, but maybe not. Justice my husband moved out.

Journey: Oh, Jania, I'm sorry. If Honesty didn't have this gift then . . .

Jania: No, it was good she revealed what was going on. I didn't know, but I'm okay. I've been selling a lot of homes and I'm doing well. So how is Love doing? She doesn't call me like she used to.

Journey: She's fine. I love her store it's so nice Jania: Oh yes, it's gorgeous.

Jania: Hi, Honesty! She is such a beautiful girl. How is she?

Journey: She's okay. She just hasn't taken her back to that school yet. You just wasted your money, you know.

Jania: No, I did not. And if she never goes, you can get that money and use it for something else; there is a refund.

Journey: Oh really? That's good to know. I was working for Love at her store and I had to quit due to Honesty not feeling well.

Jania: Oh my, really? Umm, would you and Honesty like some sweet tea?

Journey: Sure, oh and I met her daughter Faith and she is a doll.

Jania: Have you met the dad yet? He is a handsome man but got control issues.

Journey: No, and sounds like he has a lot of money. Jania: Yep, that he do have.

Journey: How did you and Love meet?

Jania: Oh, I met her when I came down here from New York for a real state meeting. Her husband Kavarri was there, so we kept in touch.

Journey: Nice. Yeah we are doing fine over there and thanks for telling her about us.

Jania: No problem, I knew you would like it there. Love needed someone to keep her company since she went through her divorce.

Journey: It's a nice place; but since her daughter lives with her now, I feel like two a crowd.

Jania: Well, if you want, you can always come here if you get uncomfortable. (they hug

Journey: Thanks for the offer. I'll be in touch. Jania: Bye, Honesty!

So we headed back home. While I was driving, Honesty grabbed my hand.

Journey: Honesty dear, let mommy drive.

As I went to turn down the main street we usually take to get home, Honesty yelled! "Don't go that way!" So I put on breaks.

Journey: Honesty, why not go this way? Then she grabbed her drawing pad and sketched a bad accident.

So I took her word for it and headed the other way. When we arrived home, there were police, news people, and ambulance down the street. I was in shock. I couldn't believe my eyes. Honesty was right. So we went into the house and turned on the news. And as I looked closely, they showed a picture of Justice, Jania's husband, and Hymns his girlfriend. I ran to the phone to call Jania.

(ringing) Jania: Hello!

Journey: Oh my God! Jania! Justice and Hymns have been in a bad accident. They are on the news, turn your TV on.

Jania: OMG! What! It is Justice. Let me call the police, bye.

Journey: Honesty, I didn't know you can also see danger ahead of time along with seeing people's dark secrets. Dear, I know you hate these gifts, but you have them for a reason.

Honesty: I hate it! I hate it! And it makes me tired when this happens, Mom. It takes my strength away.

Journey: I know, dear, but we will get through this. There has to be a cure. We may have to go out of the country to find it. Oh, Lord, help Justice and Hymns, don't let them die. (Phone rings) Hello! Is he okay? Oh no, Jania, is that what happened to her? Oh my God, and how is Justice? Oh no. Okay, just call me if you need me to come to hospital. Okay, bye.

Honesty speaking in a low tone: I know. Hymns lost her arm and Justice his leg and arm are broken.

Journey: How . . . I mean . . . OMG! Honesty, how did you know? What other gifts do you have? Honey, I don't know what you are capable of and that bothers me.

Honesty crying: I don't know why, Mom, I don't want to see things or feel or draw, and I don't want to talk because talking takes my strength too.

Journey: I'm sorry you feel like this. And it's sad that Justice and his unborn child and the mother is in this horrible accident. Now what's in store for Jania?

Honesty: Much is in store for her, Mom. It's 5:00 p.m., back at Love's store.

Faith: Okay, Mom, we are done for the day.

Love: Yes! And I'm tired and you got a birthday party to go to.

Faith: It will be fun, and I hope Honesty will have a good time. Love: I hope so because her whole life has changed. So be her friend, okay, dear. Let's go. (Cell rings) I can't get out of the parking lot before someone calls. Hello! Kavarri, why are you calling? I thought I told you not now. No! Faith and I don't want to go out to eat. Listen, I'm not doing this with you, so please stay away. (click)

Faith: That was dad, wasn't it?

Love: Yes, and he really needs to understand what he did when he ran off with you. I haven't had custody of you since the divorce and I deserve to have you now. I'm not cooking tonight so let's stop and get something.

Back at Love's house

Journey: Let me call Jania's cell. (ringing) Jania: Hello, hello!

Journey: Jania, are you on your way to the hospital? Jania: Yes, and I don't know why.

Journey: I know it's hard to go and be at his side when his girlfriend is there, but I'm sure you still have love for him and this is why you are doing it.

Jania: I guess you are right. I do still love him and I won't let this other woman stop me from seeing about him. So let me call you later. (Jania talking to herself) Oh God, be with Justice and . . . Oh God, I can't pray for her at this time, you will have to help me. Okay, let's see. The hospital is this way. Come on, light! Huh, these people. Okay, let me park. (slams door) Let's see. Oh there's the info booth. Hi, my name is Jania Henderson and I'm here to see Justice Henderson, he was in an accident.

Receptionist: Yes, he is here, but you can't go in. Jania: Why?

Receptionist: Because he has requested that if you came to not let you in.

Jania: Are you serious! He is all broken up, how can he even think to say that? Look, he must be out of his mind, he would never say that.

Receptionist: I know this comes as a surprise, but I can't let you back there to see him.

Jania: Fine, thank you. (Talking to herself) I'll just sneak back there. Let me see. Oh this door is locked. Let me try this emergency entrance, yes! Now I need to know what room. Excuse me, but my friend Justice Henderson is here, do you know what room he is in?

Nurse: Yes, just go down this hall and make a right. He is in the first room to your right.

Jania: Thank you. There it is. (whispering) OMG! Look at him, all bandage up. Justice, can you hear me? Justice, it's me Jania.

(Justice whispering: Why are you here? I told them to not let you in. Jania: Why would you say that?

Justice whispering: Because I know how you feel about her and the whole thing. (coughing)

Jania: Yes, I'm hurt, but it doesn't stop me from coming to see about you. I still will do what I have to do to help you.

Justice whispering: Then take care of my child, huh. Jania: What?

Back at Love's

Love: Journey, were home! I got Chinese. Journey says in a low voice: Hi, you two. Love: What's wrong?

Journey: Jania is at the hospital because Justice and his girlfriend were in an accident.

Love: Oh my word! Are they okay!

Journey: No, Justice's leg and arm are broken, and his girlfriend lost her arm.

Love: Sounds like that was a bad accident. I'll give Jania time and then I'll call her. Faith, you two should be getting dressed.

Journey: Poor Jania, she's up there. I know it's hard for her to see him with the other woman.

Love: I know, I couldn't do it, I just couldn't.

Journey: You mean, you would let anger keep you from helping the one you love?

Love: Yes, I'm not that strong. Jania is doing great to be there, but I couldn't do that. Besides does she still love him is the question.

Journey: Looks like you have something to work on. Well, I'm going to go help Honesty get dressed.

So I headed upstairs, and when I opened the door, Honesty was already dressed

Journey: Well, look at my beautiful girl! I love that outfit. The black top and skirt, yes, you did good. You ready?

Honesty shakes her head yes.

Journey: And promise me you will be good; no drawing, right? Honesty says in a small voice: Right.

Faith: Knock, knock. Can I come in.

Journey: Sure. Oh my, look at Faith, you look awesome.

Faith: I got jeans on. That's all of us teens wear now. Hey, Honesty, you look nice. You got your shades?

Journey: Yep, here they are. Love: Faith and Honesty, let's go. Faith: Okay, Mom. Ready.

Journey: Have a great time you two. I hope Jania is doing okay. (phone rings) Hello! Oh hi Kavarri. No, she took Faith and my daughter to a birthday party. She has her cell. Okay, bye. Wow, he doesn't stop.

He reminds me of Honesty's dad when we first met, and kind of sounds like him too. Okay, Chinese food; guess I'll eat leftovers.

Inside Love's car

Faith: Turn here, Mom. Okay, then pull in front of that red corvette. Love: And who's corvette?

Faith: My friend's dad's car. Oh, look, Isaac is here.

Love: You mean Isaac who won best supporting actor in that play you took me too?

Faith: Yes, and he likes me, ha.

Love: Okay, missy, slow down. Are the parents going to be here the whole time?

Faith: Yes, mother, they are. Come on, Honesty. Love: Call me when it's over. Bye.

Faith: OMG! Isaac is here. Okay, I must be calm. (knock knock) Tamar: Hey, Faith! Come in, and who's your friend?

Faith: This is Honesty and she lives with us.

Tamar: Hi. Well, come on let's have fun. Yahoo! (upbeat music in background)

Faith: Honesty, there is Isaac. I know you can't see him but he is handsome. OMG! He's coming over here.

Isaac: Hey, Faith! Long time no hear or see, where have you been?

Faith: I've been in Florida with my dad, but I'm back. Hey, meet my friend, Honesty. Honesty, Isaac.

Isaac: Hi! So why you wearing shades?

Faith: Oh, Honesty is blind. Yeah, it's sad but she does well. Hey

Honesty is an artist, she can sketch very good. It would be awesome if she showed off her talent by sketching Tamar and I.

Isaac: That'd be cool! Hey Tamar, come over here and let Faith friend sketch a photo of you two.

Tamar: Wow she sketches blind, this has to be the most awesome gift ever. Hey, my mom does a lot of painting I'll just get her stuff. Okay here it is go for it. As everyone stood watching with amazed eyes, Honesty drew a photo of Isaac and I kissing.

Isaac : Hey why did she draw that?

Honesty: OMG ! Honesty why did you draw this?

Honesty: Said in a low voice, because its true.

Faith: Is it true Tamar and Isaac?

Isaac: No! I mean yes.

Faith: Let's go Honesty and Tamar you aren't my friend anymore.

Isaac: Please let me take you home.

Faith: No, I'll call my mother. Come on, Honesty, let's wait down the street.

Back at Love's home, phone rings.

Love: Hello! Hi dear, you want me to pick you up? Is the party over already? Okay, I'll be there. She sound bothered.

Journey: I hope they are okay?

Love: I hope so too. Let me go, I'll be back. Back at Tamar's house

Isaac: Faith! I'm sorry, I didn't mean to kiss Tamar. I was just hurt that you left me.

Faith: It's over now. It's been revealed. Thank God, Honesty has a gift, and besides I didn't know I was moving. My father just up and moved.

Isaac: Honesty! Tell me how you knew? What are you, a seer? Or a fortune teller! Tell me!

Faith: Back off Isaac, Honesty is not to blame. You did it and that's that. My mother is here, bye.

Love: What happened?

Faith: Well, Isaac, the one you know liked me in school but I didn't want to date him because of dad. You know how he is. So while I was gone Isaac and Tamar, my girlfriend, ended up dating and it's wrong. She was my friend.

Love: Well, how did you find this out? Faith: Honesty, she told me.

Love: What you mean Honesty told you?

Faith: Well, not exactly told me with words. We asked Honesty to draw a picture of me and Tamar, but she ended up drawing Isaac and Tamar kissing. And that opened a can of worms. Tamar got mad at Isaac thinking he told Honesty something.

Love: Honesty, dear, why did you draw that picture?

Honesty (speaking in a low voice): I-I just knew he was hiding something.

Faith: You did? How strange. Your mom didn't tell me you could do that.

Love: Well, honey, just brush it under the rug. There's a special guy out there for you, just wait. We made it home, girls, and there is still a lot of Chinese food left.

Journey: Hey, how was the party? You two didn't stay long.

Love: Long story. Girls, wash up so you can eat. Hmm, it's 7:30 p.m., time flies.

Journey: What happened?

Love: Oh, there was this guy at the party who liked Faith, but comes to find out that he and a friend of Faith's had been dating. So she's upset.

Journey: How she find out?

Love: According to Faith, Honesty drew a picture of Isaac and Tamar kissing when she should have been drawing Faith and Tamar.

Journey: Really? Let me go have a little talk with Honesty.

Love: You don't need to talk with her, it's over. She didn't really do anything, but I do wonder why she does strange things. You never told me she could do things like that.

Journey: No, because I don't know. I want to see how she feels about all this, that is all.

Love: Okay, but she's been through enough. Journey: I know she has.

So I headed upstairs to talk with Honesty. I walked in and she was staring out the window.

Journey: How was the party?

Honesty spoke in a low tone voice: It was okay, until I revealed something. I have no control, Mother, so don't get mad at me. And I see it caused problems.

Journey: I know you have a gift, but you must use it to where it doesn't cause problems.

Honesty speaking softly: I can't help it, Mother. It just happens. Journey: Okay dear. Let's just go eat and hope this blows over. At 8:00 p.m. Back at the hospital.

Jania: What do you mean "take care of your child"?

Justice speaking with a raspy voice: How will I or Hymns be able to take care of our child? Huh, oh this pain.

Jania: I understand what you are saying, but I don't think I could do that. I mean, me taking care of the child you made with another woman. Would be bizarre and I don't doubt that Hymns would want that.

Justice coughing: She has no choice now. Our child will be born in a few months.

Jania: You want me to take on a newborn? You know I sell homes and you know how busy it can get.

Justice: I just want you to help us until we can get rehab. She's going to need a false arm. I just need you to help me if you can find it in your heart to do it. And Jania, we both will need to move in with you so you can help us.

Jania: What! Move in! You didn't say that, I-I got to think about this one.

Back at Love's house

Love: (phone rings) Hello, hi Semaj. You're calling pretty late. What's new? Oh really, so child support is on hold, why? You said he could set up Payments. What you mean I have only temporary custody, well he violated the order, ok I see. well, I don't feel sorry for him, my sister, or Mercy. Tell me, when will they all be doing time? Oh just probation and possibly a gross misdemeanor? Okay, thanks. (phone rings again) Hello!

Kavarri: Listen to me, I know what I did was wrong, but I only did it because I wanted to get away and start a new life. Us divorcing was hard for me and I just needed to move on without you nagging at me. But I need you to do something for me, could you please drop the charges on all of us?

Love: Why would I want to do that? You all brought this on yourselves.

Kavarri: Come on! Love, you got her back she's with you so just drop the charges. If I get probation and a gross misdemeanor I'm not paying you child support and you know you can use that for our daughter. I leave that with you, bye.

Journey: Hey, you look puzzled.

Love: I am, I found out that if Kavarri gets probation and a gross Misdemeanor he wont pay me child support and I could use that money to put Faith through college. He, Mercy, and my sister deserve what's coming to them but I may just drop the charges.

Journey: I think that's fair and your sister and Mercy will love you.

Love: I didn't say I would do that for them even though Kavarri ask me to. I don't know, it's a hard one, I'll have to think this over. I'm going to bed; it's been a long day.

Faith: Mom, Auntie Hope is on the phone.

Love: Tell her I'm tired and I don't feel like talking to her. Faith: Oh, you heard her okay. Love you, Auntie Hope. Bye. Love: Faith, come here please.

Faith: Yes.

Love: If your auntie asks any questions, just tell her she has to ask me, okay?

Faith: Okay, and I need to sign up for school and then after school I can work at the store.

Love: Well, like you said, I was just giving you time to rest from all that had happened, but I was thinking homeschooling.

Faith: Oh, Mother, then I wouldn't be able to play sports or anything else with my friends.

Love: Okay fine. In the morning I'll sign you up. Umm, did you ever go to school in Florida?

Faith: No, I was in hiding. Ha ha. Dad had me homeschooled. You two think alike.

Love: Please don't say that. Okay, bed time. See you in the morning. (Talking to herself) I don't know if I should drop these charges, but if I don't then I won't get child support and that will be a waste. Let me go to bed and think about this.

At 7:00 a.m.

Journey: Morning is here and I have no job. I wish I could start my own business. Oh well, (yawning) I smell coffee.

Love: Yes, it's brewing. How did you sleep last night?

Journey: I slept well. I was thinking about a home business since I got Honesty to deal with.

Love: What kind of business?

Journey: Well, something where Honesty can do portraits for weddings, birthdays, etc. It would be nice since she loves to draw.

Love: Remember we talked about this before? It's a great idea and plus, I know people I can tell. You see how everyone wanted me to draw them.

Journey: Yeah, but I don't know when. So have you thought it over if you are going to drop the charges?

Love: I think I will, but he will have to sign something. I will tell him later. I got to take Faith to the school to sign up.

Journey: Okay, I'll just eat something and wait for Honesty to wake up. I may get her in school also. Jania said I could use the money if I didn't want to put her in that school, and that was two thousand.

Love: Sounds good. It's up to you.

Journey: I may just go and get the money and put it in the bank for hard times. It's been a while since I had a bank account.

Love going upstairs: Sounds good again.

Journey: I hope Jania is doing okay. I may call her later. First, I will get dressed. Let's see, it's 7:45 a.m., shower time.

Love: Faith! Are you up? Faith: Yes, I'm getting dressed.

Love: Okay, I'm getting in the shower. (cell rings) OMG! I can't get anything done. Hello! Oh, hi, Hope.

Hope: I'm calling to see if you are going to drop the charges. Kavarri said you were.

Love: He said that? Well, I've been thinking, I will have to talk with my lawyer and I will get back to all of you.

Hope: I just don't want to lose my job over this. For me, to be on probation and have a gross misdemeanor would ruin my and Denali's reputation, and I don't need that.

Love: I will see what my lawyer says. But what you did by keeping this a secret from me was wrong. Just know that. Bye. Oh gosh! Maybe I can take a shower now.

Faith: Mom, hurry! Thirty minutes later.

Journey: Morning, Faith. I hear you're on your way to sign up for school.

Faith: Yes, I'm ready to get back on the honor roll.

Journey: I remember when Honesty was in school, she was always receiving awards for her art work.

Faith: She is a great artist after seeing that picture of Isaac and Tamar, ha. She's the best.

Journey: Yes, Honesty has a lot of surprises up her sleeve. Love: I'm ready.

Journey: Okay, bye you guys. (Phone ringing) Hello! Hi, Jania! How are ya?

Jania: I'm exhausted and stressed out. Justice is asking too much of me.

Journey: Like what?

Jania: Like let him and his girlfriend stay with me until they both get well, and I can't take on that responsibility. And they have a baby coming.

Journey: So the baby is okay?

Jania: Yes, the baby is fine. But I can't do it. How could I handle that? She, the-the woman whom my husband cheated on me with, living in my home?

Journey: It's a tough one. I don't know what to say.

Jania: They both will be in the hospital for a while, so I have time to think about this.

Journey: Well, if you need my help just call me, okay? Jania: Okay, thanks. Bye.

Journey: Bye. Honesty, oh you scared me, how did you sleep? Honesty speaking in a low voice: I had a dream and I drew it. See.

Journey: Oh my. So that's why Kavarri wants to stall time, that game player. Here we go again, I have to find out how to tell Love, I'll talk to her when she gets back. In the meantime, Honesty, let's go to the blind school.

So we left the house; and as I was driving I was thinking of going to get the money so I can open a bank account so that we would have emergency funds. We made it here.

Journey: Let's go in and see what we can do. Hello, I'm Journey . . . Receptionist: Oh yes, I remember you. How may I help you?

Journey: Well, as you know that my friend Jania paid for my daughter's first six months, and she told me that if I didn't want to put my daughter in school that I could get the money back.

Receptionist: Oh sure, a refund. And may I ask why you don't want her to start school?

Journey: Well, my daughter has been through so much since she became blind, and it calls for me to be by her side daily. But I'm thinking about homeschooling for her.

Receptionist: That's an exception so here is your receipt, and God bless you both.

Journey: Thanks, and bless you too.

So our next stop will be the bank. I just wanted to get this over with and like I said, I'm thinking about homeschooling for you Honesty. It just would be safer. Okay, the bank wasn't that far. Here it is. Wow, a lot of people here. Let's sit over there and wait for someone to come.

Banker: Hello, may I help you?

Journey: Yes, I'm here to open up a new account.

Banker: Sure, follow me. Have a seat. Back at Love's shop

Love: Huh, I'm glad that is over now. It's time to get to work. Let's see, today is Friday and you start school Monday, good.

Faith: Hey, Mom, I get out of school at 2:00 p.m., so I could work till closing.

Love: Sure, we close at 5:00 p.m., so yes dear, you'll make a little money. Oh boy, here comes the crowd. Hello, everyone, we have new arrivals. So please feel free to check them out. (cell ringing) Hello, Kavarri, what can I do for you? What! No, I will not let Mercy work here, and you got your nerve asking me that. No, you already want me to drop charges, now you want me to give her job back? I'm not being mean; I said no and that's that. Bye. Oh, God, help me. Yes, I said it. God, I do believe you are there, just bear with me until I start trusting in you.

Faith: Mom, that lady just brought a whole rack of those little gold cats, and they priced at $50.

Love: We are doing well, and you'll be able to go to college.

Faith: And I know what I want to be, and that is a lawyer. Then I can help people who are low income. Pro bono is what I will do for many.

Love: Give me a hug. I'm proud too of you. I guess you growing up with money didn't close your eyes to the needy. Good girl.

Faith: Well, Mom, money isn't everything; but family and helping people is.

Love: Happy to hear that too. Well, why don't you run across the street and get us lunch.

Faith: What do you want?

Love: Surprise me. Back at the bank

Journey: I'm so glad I got this done. Now with the CD I got for us, I can roll over whatever it accumulates, right?

Banker: Oh, yes, you can do that or put the interest in savings, and we will send out letters letting you know when your maturity is up.

Journey: Okay, thanks for your help. Let's get home. At the hospital

Jania: Justice, I got to go. I just came by to see how you were doing.

Justice: Listen, are you going to let me and her move in or not? I'm in too much pain to keep asking you, so please answer me.

Jania: I will have to think about it, and besides you are going to be here for at least three weeks and her maybe more. So don't keep asking me. Give me time, and while you are here think about what you are asking me to do, bye. (talking to self) Oh, my life is so crazy. I have homes to sell; I got to go home, and lie down. (beep, beep) Move out of my way! Where do these people learn to drive?

Kavarri calling Mercy Mercy: Hello.

Kavarri: Hey, how's it going? Good. Hey, have you found a job yet? You haven't. Well, I'm just calling to let you know I will get you a job and I will put some money in your account.

Mercy: Thanks. I need money, but I don't expect you to keep supporting me.

Kavarri: Yeah, well, I got you fired so what else can I do but pay your way.

Mercy: You're not hurting for nothing anyway. People call you all the time asking you to contract with them.

Kavarri: It's been slow though, and I have been focusing on Love dropping the charges. You understand that if she doesn't this could mess up our reputation The least that can happen is being put on probation, the worse is having a gross misdemeanor and I definitely don't want that on my record. So maybe you should call Love and beg her to drop the charges just like I did.

Mercy: No! I will not. You are doing a great job of it, and besides you got us into this; so you deal with it. Bye (click)

Kavarri: Women, why do I even deal with them? Back at Love's house

Journey: Good, we are home. We now have a bank account, and I'm thinking you should do home school, dear, just for a few months. See, here I can be with you to where if you were in a class setting and something happen I wouldn't know how to deal with it. So let me think on this for a while. Sweetie, why don't you lay down and rest, you need that to keep going. I'm going to cook while you rest. (phone rings) Hello? Excuse me! Who is this? Love doesn't want you calling. What! You called me! Please don't call here. (click) Oh my God, I can't believe people. Honesty dear, I thought you went to lay down.

Honesty: Mercy.

Journey: Yes, what about her, how, oh why I even ask. Honesty: She will pay for that.

Journey: Well, I don't like what she said! She said . . . Honesty: That you are a slut.

Journey: Now look, Honesty, you can't let what someone said make you want to hurt them, so don't do anything stupid. Your unusual gift is not for hurting people, so just calm down.

Honesty: My gift is not to hurt anyone, Mother; I just draw what I see.

Journey: And wha-what do you see for her? Honesty: (silent)

Door slams

Love: Hi, Journey, how was your day?

Journey: It was good. I finally got a bank account.

Love: Oh really? Good for you, and I finally signed Faith up for school. She will be working at the store after school.

Journey: I'm glad you have help because I couldn't help you and

Mercy is no longer with you so Faith will be a big help.

Love: I'm just struggling with calling my lawyer about dropping charges.

Journey: Umm, speaking of that, right after you told me about dropping charges I was thinking maybe you are making a mistake.

Love: What do you mean?

Journey: Well, when I was in the shelter, there were women there who talked about how their ex-husbands acted like they really cared for them just so they could get custody.

Love: He couldn't do that, not after what just happened. The court would never give her back to him, no way.

Journey: It's not like he can't try.

Love: I'm not worried. Bottom line he is going to have to pay child support, and all I know I'm struggling with not putting him in ail, because if he is in jail he can't work and his clientele will go down. As you may know, when they pay, it helps our kids. Now you may not care but I do. I'm done with this conversation.

Journey: Have it your way. (talking to self) She will see if she doesn't Make sure the court give him probation and a gross misdemeanor. I really hope the judge don't fall for his story.

Love: Let me call Jania and see what she says about this. (ringing) Jania sounding tired: Hello.

Love: Hello, Jania, how are you? Jania: Who is this?

Love: It's Love! You sound sick, are you okay? Jania: Oh, Journey didn't tell you?

Love: Tell me what?

Jania: About how Justice want me to let him and that woman of his live with me until they both get well.

Love: I heard a little, but are you going to do it? I mean that's going too far. How could he ask you that? I never heard of someone asking this, what are you going to do?

Jania: I don't know. Enough about me, how are things going with you?

Love: Oh it's been crazy. I mean, work and court and lawyers, yeah my life is crazy.

Jania: What you mean courts and lawyer?

Love: Oh, Journey didn't tell you? Jania: Tell me what?

Love: Oh, to make a long story short . . . (At Kavarri's lawyer's office)

Kavarri: Listen, Eli, I need to get custody of my daughter and I'll pay you good to find away.

Eli: Look, I have done many twists for you but this is different. The judge has the last say. I mean, you ran off and you didn't even tell her you were leaving, let alone me.

Kavarri: Man! Man! Now I got to pay her child support, I don't mind but I hate paying it to her.

Eli: I know this is very frustrating, but either way you will have a gross misdemeanor, probation on your record and child support to pay.

Kavarri: Look, just get me out if this mess.

Eli: That will be up to Love to drop the charges.

Kavarri: Yes and no. Yes, it will be up to her and no it's not all up to her. I pay you to help me and that's what I expect. Now here is twenty-five thousand, and when she says she is not dropping the charges, you do something about it or give me my money back. I will be waiting for your call.

Eli: I will be ready for her, see you soon. Kavarri: Yeah. (door slams)

(Back at Love's phone conversation)

Love: And that's the hell I been through, Jania.

Jania: Oh, Love, I didn't even know, and Journey wasn't going to tell me your business. But we both have been through a lot, ha. I remember when we used to go everywhere to just hang out.

Love: I know, it's all over now, but I think I will drop the charges.

Jania: Just make sure your lawyer have Kavarri to sign something stating he won't try anything funny.

Love: Don't worry, I will make sure of that. But back to your problem, if I was you I couldn't do it, but if you find it in your heart to do it, then peace to you.

Jania: Thanks, Love, I'm going to lay down.

Love: Okay, take care. Well, I will call my lawyer in the morning, bed time for me.

(At 1:00 a.m., Honesty was up, drawing and whispering.) Honesty: Twenty-five thousand, twenty-five thousand Repeat.

Journey yawning: Honesty dear, what are you doing up drawing. Honesty: Twenty-five thousand

It's pitched dark, I can't see. I cut on the light and walked over to see what she was drawing; and when I looked, it was a picture of a man giving another man money, but neither had a face. So I just overlooked it and told Honesty to lay down and she did. I noticed she was sweating even though the air condition was on.

(At 7:00 a.m.)

Love: Faith! Are you up? It's time for school. Faith: I've been up, Mom, and I ate breakfast.

Love: Okay, let's go. I got to make a stop.

(Water running)

Journey yawning: Oh boy, let me take a shower while Honesty is still asleep.

(In Love's car)

Faith: Mom, are you going to drop the charges?

Love: I don't think so. He needs to pay for what he did. And court is pretty soon, so . . . let him deal with it. Listen, honey, your father should have thought about what he was doing. Now he has to reap what he sowed.

Faith: Mom, that's not nice. He is still my dad. Why can't you two just stop it! I hate this.

(Pulls into school parking lot) (cell phone rings)

Love: Hello, yes this is her. Who is this? Bye, dear, see you after school. Excuse me sir, Eli, who? Oh, this is my ex-husband's lawyer. Okay, so why are you calling me? Oh, meet with me. Okay, let's meet at that nice café here in town. Oh, and what will you be wearing? Okay, fine see you soon. Hmm, I wonder what he is up to? (Arrived at cafe)

Eli talking to self: I hope my plot works. Hello, Love. Love: How did you know?

Eli: I only have a picture of you in your ex-husband's file. Please have a seat.

Love: I really shouldn't be talking to you. I mean you are my enemy.

But I want to hear what you have to say.

Eli: You are right, I am your enemy, yet I think you will like what I have to say. Look, we both know that what your ex-husband did was wrong. But I feel he shouldn't have to have those two changes on him and be away from his daughter. I hate when fathers are apart from their kid's life. How do you feel about that?

Love: Well . . . I . . . well, I feel the same but . . .

Eli: But you are mad and angry and you want revenge like all the rest of us. But is that right? No, it's not.

Love: I realized that if Kavarri get probation and a gross misdemeanor, he would fight me tooth and nail to not give me child support I would not get child support, So I been thinking maybe I should drop the charges.

Eli: Ha, I mean what he did was wrong, and I have never done this, but I agree, he should do time but the charges that he got will suffice.

Love: What! You agree? Yeah, I agree too, but I want my child support, therefore I will drop the charges.

Eli: Listen, I've been Kavarri's lawyer for five years, and I'm sick and tired of how he just throws his money around and calls the shots. Tell me this, if you had ten thousand right now, would that help you out? I mean, I know that when we go to court, the charges would just be a slap on the wrist. But he needs to learn his lesson. And when we settle how much he will pay you in child support, it will be four thousand a month. So if you had ten thousand, I'm sure that will get you through until he gets out.

Love: Yes, if I had ten thousand that would help, but I don't.

Eli: You do now.

Love: Whoa! Why are you giving me this?

Eli: I told you, Kavarri needs to pay for what he has done. If he can keep paying people off he will never learn. He doesn't know this, but after court I will no longer be his lawyer. I can't deal with him anymore. So take this money and let him get his charges along with the other two.

Love: Huh, I guess I could use this money now. How do I know I can trust you?

Eli: Put it like this, it will be my word against yours. Just keep this between us. If anyone finds out we did this, we both will be locked up; so never ever tell a soul.

Love: Thanks, and I won't say a word. Eli: Hey, let me leave first.

Love: Okay, bye. Wow, what did I just do? Then again who cares what I just did. Kavarri needs to learn he can't just take my daughter and cause me to suffer. I will not drop the charges.

(Back at Love's house)

Journey: Honesty, dear are you okay? Honesty, answer me. You must be tired, because you were up early drawing a man with money. Tell me who is that?

Honesty: I don't know.

Journey: Okay, I won't keep asking, but you and I know you don't do this and it doesn't mean anything. Let me call Love and see if she is okay. (cell rings)

Love: Hello? Oh hey, Journey, how are you? No, I'm not driving while talking. I'm at the café. What's up, my dear? No, I haven't opened the store yet, and I'm sure my customers are mad at me, ha, but I'm leaving to go there now. Yeah, I'm fine. Hey, why don't you and Honesty stop by the store? Okay, bye.

Journey: (sigh) (Jania's phone rings)

Jania: Hello? Yes, this is her. Oh okay, thank you for calling. Bye.

Oh God! Why am I even going to see what Justice wants? Why me?

(Love's store, at 9:30 a.m.)

Love: Oh gosh, look at the line! Hello! Everyone, I had an emergency but I'm here. Come on in. Hi, Silent, I'm glad you stopped by. How's the kids?

Silent: They are doing fine, but I'm not. Peter is back to drinking and I got to talk to our pastor. How about you? How are things going?

Love: I'm good. I'm divorced from Kavarri, but I have Faith and that's all that matters. Oh and I got the store here to keep me going.

Silent: Well, I must say you have a nice store with a lot of nice things. Hey, I got to run, but I'll stop by sometime so we can just sit and chat.

Love: That will be great. Hey, wait, are you still a manager at that modelling company?

Silent: Yes, why?

Love: Oh, because I need help in the mornings, and Faith comes after she gets out of school; but that's not until 2:00 p.m.

Silent: Well, I can come on weekends.

Love: Oh, well, just stay in touch with me okay.

Silent: All right, let me check out these candles you have before I go. Love: Kavarri, what are you doing here?

Kavarri at store: Tell me, are you going to drop the charges? Love: No, I'm not so . . . leave.

Kavarri: What did you say?

Love: I said, no, I'm not dropping the charges so please leave my store.

Kavarri: You are a selfish devil, but you will pay for this.

Love: And you will too, bye. (talking to self) I can't believe him coming to my store. Huh, the nerve of that man.

Journey: Love! Hey!

Love: I see you two made it, how are you?

Journey: We're okay. It's nice to get out of the house. Hey, let me buy us lunch later.

Love: Can you afford it? I mean, I don't want you spending a dime if you don't have to.

Journey: Look, you and Jania had been great to me. I mean, you've been paying for everything, and I don't know how to repay you.

Love: Well, there is one thing you can do. Journey: What-what, anything.

Love: I know you say you got to take care of Honesty, but I was wondering if you could start back helping me here at the store.

Journey: I can do that. It's just that Honesty doesn't sleep well at night and when morning comes, she is too drained. But I can work around that.

Love: I will figure it out. Let me help this customer. (At the hospital)

Jania: Well, I'm here. (elevator door closes) (elevator door opens) Hi, I'm here to see Justice.

Nurse: Sure. Jania: Hi.

Justice: Hi. I see you made it, what took you so long.

Jania: Excuse me. You may be in pain but I'm in pain too, if you haven't noticed. So what did you want?

Justice coughing: Well, you know, I haven't been working and . . . I need your help.

Jania: Oh my God! I can't believe you. I mean, you cheated on me and you get her pregnant, then after all this you want me to let you and your mistress move in with me until you both get well? Now you need me to help you with money.

Justice: Look, I took care of you and gave you many things; and that home you are in, I brought for you. And you know what, I don't want it. Remember all that money you have I haven't fought for it, I let you have it all. And I ask for help and you can't give it to me.

Jania: Yeah, I guess I can help you. Sure, what do you need? Justice: I need twenty thousand and I know you got it. Remember, we had a joint account

Jania: Wait. You got plenty of money, so why do you need me to help you?

Justice: Because I can't get to it. You know me, I have to go through offshore banks. I will pay you back.

Jania: Okay, where is the payment going?

Justice: I need twenty thousand and I need it to go to the IRS. Jania: IRS! You haven't been paying taxes? We could lose everything. Oh my God!

Justice: Will you stop it! Huh, I-I can't fight with you. Tell the nurse I need a pain pill, please.

Jania: Sure. (door closes) (Outside Love's store) Kavarri: (calling Eli) Eli: Hi, this is Eli.

Kavarri: Well, tell me some good news. Eli: What you mean good news?

Kavarri: You know I paid you! To keep me out so I can get my daughter?

Eli: Listen, I haven't even gotten that far yet. I should speak with her lawyer soon.

Kavarri: Her lawyer! Why her lawyer?

Eli: Because this is what lawyers do, and I can try and cut a deal with him. But I don't know if it will work.

Kavarri: And if it doesn't work, I want my money back, you got it!

Eli: Mr. Kavarri, you seem to have forgotten that you have to pay for my services.

Kavarri: And have you forgotten that if you do a poor job then I can get my money back and I will. I know people.

Eli: You are not working with me. This law stuff takes time and as we all know, the judge has the last say.

Kavarri: Listen to me and listen good. I don't care about the judge. Just let me know before court the good news. Oh, and court is when?

Eli: Court is in one week.

Kavarri: Man, I need to get out of this. At least get me a warning.

Eli: I will see what the judge says. Kavarri: Sounds good, talk later. (phone hangs up) (Back at Love's store)

Faith: Hi, Mom.

Love: Hi, honey, how was school?

Faith: It was fun, and I signed up to be a cheerleader. Love: Wonderful, honey.

Faith: Hey, Mom, where's Honesty? Love: Oh, she's in the back office.

Faith: Okay, I'll go back there and see what she is doing. Hey! (voice fades) What have you done? Why you write ten thousand on the wall?

Honesty: silent

Faith: Answer me! Mom is going to be very upset that you wrote on her wall. Why did you do this?

Honesty: Silent Faith: Mom! Mom!

Honesty: Don't call her in here.

Faith: I think you need help. This is not cool.

Honesty: You signed up to be a cheerleader. Well, I hope you make it.

Faith: What do you mean, hope I make it? I'm good at it. Honesty: So is the girl flower. Do you know her?

Faith: What? Yes, I know her. How can I forget? She's the one who beat me in track. This is crazy, are you a mind reader?

Honesty: silent

Faith: All I know is that you are in deep trouble. Mom! Love: What dear, why are you yelling in the store?

Faith: Come. Look.

Love: Oh my God! Honesty, why did you write ten thousand on the wall?

Honesty: silent Love: Answer me. Honesty: silent

Journey: What is going on here? Honesty are you all right?

Faith: When I came back here to talk to her, she had written ten thousand all over the wall.

Love: Why has she done this? This is strange. Journey: Why is it strange? You know she is not well. Love: Well, I-I mean it's strange she would do that.

Journey: This is what I mean when I say I have to take care of her. My life has changed since Honesty became blind and it takes a toll on me.

Love: I understand. I will meet you at the house. Journey: Very well. Come on, Honesty, let's go. Faith: Mom, I don't think Honesty is normal.

Love: Yeah, something is strange about her. You know one time, she grabbed my hand and started drawing a picture, and that was scary. But looking back, it seem like after I drew the picture of Mercy and Hope, I found out they were part of your being missing. Strange again.

Faith: Really, Mom? Wow, that was weird. I hope she is okay to live with us.

Love: Me too. We'll talk later. Let's get to work; we only got three more hours to go. Go see what that lady wants over there. (talking to self) Honesty wrote ten thousand. Hmm, I wonder what she meant. Why would she write that same amount that Eli gave me. She doesn't know him. Something is fishy.

(Journey in the car with Honesty)

Journey: Honesty, that was a stupid thing you did, and what is up with this ten thousand?

Honesty speaking low: I don't know, I just do what comes to me. Journey: Honey, this has to stop. I can't afford to move right now. Honesty: I can't stop it, Mom! I can't.

Journey: Did you have to write on the wall?

Honesty: I didn't know I did that, Mother. I-I can't control my hands and mind.

Journey: We're almost home and you can lay down. Honesty: Eli!

Journey: Who is Eli?

Honesty: I don't know, but he is connected to the ten thousand.

Journey: Oh my. Well, don't say anything to anyone, and you writing ten thousand on the wall didn't help.

Honesty: I know mother, but Love and Eli are connected. Journey: Are they? I wonder what is going on. Well, we are home; now go rest.

Honesty: I'll do some drawing that relaxes me. Journey: Okay, but for a moment.

So we went in the house. Honesty went upstairs and as she was going up she ran swiftly, I couldn't believe my eyes. So I started to look for something to cook. But for some reason, I started to think about Honesty's father, wondering where he is. I wonder why Honesty hasn't saw anything on him. I guess because she only reveals people sins and secrets.

Journey: Oh well, Honesty honey! What are you doing? (Honesty at the top of stairs)

Honesty: I was drawing.

Journey: Okay, but I want you to rest. Honesty: I will.

So I went back to looking for something to cook for dinner. And I heard Honesty scream. So I ran upstairs, and when I got up there, she had her hand over her mouth, with a shocked look on her face.

Honesty: (pointing)

Journey: When I looked at the drawing, it was Mercy holding some papers. I asked Honesty what does this mean?

Honesty low voice: I-I-don't know. It seems like Mercy is planning something.

Journey: Planning something. Hmm, like what?

Honesty: I don't know. I can't get it, but Love needs to be warned. (Back at hospital)

Justice: That pill did help. Look, thanks for helping me. I never thought it would come to this. I mean I messed up what we had and I regret it. I know you were a great wife and I just got caught up and I don't know how that happened. I think when a man is away from home, a lot of anything can happen. Women also make it hard for a man to be faithful even though he doesn't want to be unfaithful.

Jania: What you mean they make it hard?

Justice: Well, how they dress and smell good wearing perfume, how they walk and even though you have all that at home you still can be drawn away. But I'm sure, if a man would keep his mind and eyes on who he is with and don't let work and stress get the best of him, he won't mess up a good thing.

Jania: Wow, you said a mouthful, but I'm still going to have problems letting you and her move in with me.

(Phone rings)

Justice: Can you answer that?

Jania: Hello, Justice's room. No, he's right here. Here, it's your girlfriend. See you later.

Justice: Hey, don't forget to pay that?

Jania: Sure.

Justice: Hey, how are you? How's the baby? Good. Oh that was Jania. She came up here because I asked her to come, so I can have her do something for me. Hey, calm down. Neither you nor I can do too much for ourselves now, and besides you know we are moving in with her, so get used to her being around. You don't have nowhere else to go, do you? Okay then. I'm not in the mood for getting upset, so we will talk later. Bye. (click)

(Love's store)

Faith: Mom, are you going to let Journey and Honesty keep staying with us? I mean after writing on the wall, I'm a little afraid.

Journey: I know, dear, she can make you feel that way, but I just can't tell them to get out. I mean that would be unkind. I'm sure when Journey is ready to move she will move. Now let's lock up.

(Mercy's home)

Mercy talking to self: So fire me, huh. Well, I got something on her. If I can't work, then I'll just close her down, or at least try. (cell rings) Hello?

Kavarri: Hey, Mercy, how are you?

Mercy: I'm okay. I've been waiting to hear from you. Have you found me a job yet? I'm tired of living off the money you gave me; I'm used to working.

Kavarri: Haven't you been saving? I mean, you had two jobs and the store was just part time right? What happened to the other job?

Mercy: My other job, I had to resign because I didn't want this court thing to mess that up.

Kavarri: Understood. So if that's the case, then why am I trying to get you a job? I mean you should wait.

Mercy: I guess. But can't you get me a under-the-table job?

Kavarri: I can, but I don't work like that; and I've been focusing on my case and trying to keep these charges off me. Love may drop the charges on you and Hope, but me I don't know what she will do for me. So, I'm trying to stay out. Besides, I know this leader who is very powerful in his country, and he wanted me to join his organization. If I did, I would get all the support I need.

Mercy: Sounds like a cult . . . "join." That doesn't sound too good.

Kavarri: No, it's not a cult. But I need to contact him to get me out of this, but I may be too late. His name is Saul and he is powerful.

Mercy: Well, you know you are my best friend and I would do anything for you even if it meant keeping her out of the way until court is over, if you know what I mean.

Kavarri: Ha, you are becoming a little evil. I don't know if that is a good idea. I mean you don't need to add to your problem.

Mercy: She wouldn't even know it's me.

Kavarri: I don't want to hurt Faith, and that would.

Mercy: I know it would, but it wouldn't be forever; it would be until court is over.

Kavarri: Are you thinking clearly? Then when she is released she can still run to the court and carry on with her charges. Don't forget it!

Mercy: It was a thought. Well, you can walk around on eggshells, but I'm not going to jail without getting revenge.

Kavarri: I'll talk to you later. In the meantime, just wait until we see what happens in court before you get a job.

Mercy: Sure, but I need money now. I got student loans to pay, and I need my own place. I'm getting tired of living with my parents.

Kavarri: I'll send you a check for three thousand, put that in your bank, use what you need and save the rest, just in case. Hey, I just thought about something, you and Hope don't have a lawyer representing you.

Mercy: Yeah, we do, yours.

Kavarri: Oh right, I got you guys into this mess. Mercy: Okay, thanks for the cash and I'll see you later.

Kavarri: Yeah. (talking to self) Man, oh man, I got to call my lawyer. (ringing) Hey, Eli . . . umm, I need to know, are you going to help my ex-sister-in-law and my friend Mercy?

Eli: Are you paying me to do that? I mean, I work for you not them, but if you want me to represent them, then I need m-o-n-e-y.

Kavarri: Okay, okay, I'll drop a check for four thousand. Just get them off the hook. See ya.

Eli: (talking to self) Let me call Love. (dialing) (ringing) Love, how are things going?

Love: It's going. What are you calling for? Eli: You remember our deal, right?

Love: Yes, I remember.

Eli: Okay, well, Kavarri just called me and he is dropping off a check for four thousand to get your sister and Mercy off the hook. I can do that, but I won't do it for him.

Love: Well, I don't want them off; and Kavarri can get what's coming to him while he pays child support.

Eli: Okay let me work on this.

Love: You do that.

Eli: Kavarri is in for a surprise. I just want to teach him that his money can't always get him out of trouble.

Love: I like that, I've been wanting to show him that for years. Eli: Okay, I will see you in court. Bye. (click)

(Back at Jania's house) (car door slams)

Jania: (talking to self) What a day! Huh, I'm so drained. Let me sit down for a minute. Well, let's see, I know when Justice and his girl move in, I'm not going to want to be close to her so I'll give her the room down the hall. And Justice, oh, I don't know. Oh God, help me to do this. (Phone rings) Hello! Hi, Journey, how are you?

Journey: I'm fine, but how are you and Justice doing?

Jania: Don't even ask, I was just there; he had wanted me to come up so I can make a payment for him. Then while I was there his mistress called and I answered and I felt stupid.

Journey: Why, you had him first. She was just his mistress. Jania: Soon to be wife. Oh, whatever.

Journey: Well, he messed up, but now you can move on. I did when Honesty's dad left off to work out of town and never came back. I think it was a good paying job he had got.

Jania: It's going to take a long time for me to get over this. I mean, they are going to be living with me until they both get well. I can just scream.

Journey: Why don't you go see a therapist, no really, that will help you a lot.

Jania: I should. I think I will when they move in, that's when I'll need it. Well, I'll talk to you later. I got to rest, I have two buyers to meet tomorrow.

Journey: Hey, are you afraid to be in that big house by yourself? Maybe you need a dog.

Jania: I love being by myself. I'm okay, and besides Justice is coming here next week so I better enjoy the peace.

Journey: Okay get some rest, bye. Jania: Bye. (click)

Journey: Poor woman. (Front door slams)

Love: We're home, and I don't smell food cooking ha.

Journey: Well, it's so much food here. I don't know what to cook.

Love: How about I order beef BBQ ribs dinner? There is a restaurant I know of and it's perfect, you will like it.

Journey: If you want. Hi, Faith, how was school?

Faith: It was fun. Just glad to be back in school so I can graduate and go to college.

Journey: You got a good head on your shoulders. You can be successful like your mom.

Love: I hope she does. (laughing) Let me call the BBQ place. Journey: I'll go upstairs and check on Honesty. (opens door)

Honesty, how you feel, honey? I need to hide that picture of Mercy, so Love and Faith won't see it, okay.

Honesty: (Silent)

Journey: Okay and Love is ordering BBQ dinner. I want you to eat, and then we can turn in early, okay?

Honesty: I want to eat up here.

Journey: That's fine, just rest until dinner gets here.

So I went back downstairs. As I was coming down, the phone was ringing.

Journey: I'll get it, Love! Hello, yes this is Journey. Who's trying to contact me? Let me get a pen. Okay, I'm ready. Well, thanks for calling. Bye.

Love: Who was that?

Journey: It was the shelter, and they said that the social security left me a message to contact them.

Love: Sounds important. Journey: I'll call them tomorrow. (Someone knocking on door) Love: It's dinner! Hi, how much?

Delivery man: That will be sixty dollars even.

Love: Here's a hundred, and keep the change. Bye. It smells good. Journey: Are these people from the south?

Love: Yes, and they are great cooks. Oh yeah, Faith ccome eat. Journey: Oh, Honesty wants to eat upstairs, is that okay?

Love: Sure, that's fine. You can eat with her if you like.

Journey: Okay. I think it has something to do with writing on the wall.

Faith: She'll be okay.

Love: That's nice of you to say that, dear. Okay, let's eat.

Journey: I got Honesty's plate and mine. We may turn in early. I can still help you at the store, but I will have to come in at 11:00 a.m.

Love: That's fine. Then Faith will be there at 2:00 p.m., so yeah it will all work out.

(Three hours later)

Love: Oh boy, I'm tired. Faith, I don't want you to be late for school.

So go to bed and no talking on the phone.

Faith: I know, Mom, and I'm never late. Oh, I'm getting a ride from Star; she's the head cheerleader.

Love: Are you trying to get into that so you can see boys play ball?

Faith: No, Mom. It's just fun even though I will see all the boys. Goodnight, Mom.

Love: Goodnight, dear. (talking to self) Huh, life is so hard. I wonder how Jania is doing. I got to check on her; and I have court, oh God, next week and Kavarri, Hope and Mercy will get the charges they deserve. Oh my, this should be fun to watch. (phone rings) Hello, hello? Oh, Mercy, what can I do for you?

Mercy: I'm calling because I can't believe you fired me over something so small. I worked for you and ran your store with great customer service and you fired me!

Love: Look! What you did to me, your manager, while you were working for me, that was wrong. Tell me, would an employee who wanted to keep their job even get involved? You think about it, and if you don't want jail time, then I suggest you leave me alone.

Mercy: Just to let you know, I remember when you forged my name to get your store until you paid back taxes off, and I still have a copy. Do you remember that?

Love: Go ahead and try to get my store closed down and you will go to jail. I'm the one who has the say, so if you and Hope don't want to see the inside of the jail then back off! Don't make me put you there. Now after you get your charges, I may reconsider giving you your job back. It's getting late, so bye. (click) (Love taking to self) That Mercy got her nerve trying to use what I did years ago. Whatever. She just went along with it because she wanted a job. I see now, well, I'm not giving in.

Faith: Mom, you still up.

Love: Yes, but I'm going to bed now, why?

Faith: I saw your light on and I heard you yelling at someone. Was that dad again?

Love: (laughing) No, dear, it was a friend of mine. That's how we talk, no big deal. See you in the morning.

(At 6:00 a.m.)

Journey (talking to self): It's six already. (yawning) Shower time. So I got in the shower and got dressed. By this time it was 9:00 a.m. and I needed to call social security. I wonder why they were looking for me for. So I called them. (dialing)

Journey: Hello, my name is Journey Brown, and I'm trying to find out who called me. No, they didn't leave a name. Yes, I'll hold. Hmm . . . hmm . . . Yes, this is Miss Brown. Yes . . . yes . . . I never thought about drawing SSI. Yes, I had to quit my job because I hurt my back. Well, I'm glad to know I can. Oh really, my daughter can draw SSI too. Nice to know, thanks for the information. Bye.

Love: Morning! I heard you talking, but I didn't want to make any noise. You look happy.

Journey: Yes, I am. I didn't know that I could get SSI for Honesty and I. No one ever told me and we've been trying to make ends meet.

Love: Well, yes you can draw SSI. It may take a while to get, but you will get it.

Journey: I like to work, but I can sign Honesty up. Love: Hey, I would. There's a lot of help out there.

Journey: Yeah, I see there is. Tell me, have you figured out what you are going to say in court?

Love: I-I think I'm going to drop charges on my sister and Mercy, but Kavarri, he can get the charges he deserves.

Journey: Are you serious? What will Faith think? And how will you face her?

Love: Oh, there are ways to make it look like I had nothing to do with it. Lawyers lie, right?

Journey: What do you think you will gain from this, and I thought you wanted child support or has that changed?

Love: Kavarri will get the charges, and I'll get my money soon enough. As you know I can survive.

Journey: Have it your way.

Love: Oh, I will. Faith, let's go! See you later, Journey. (Door slams)

Journey: Something isn't right about her. She wanted child support and now she's acting like it means nothing. Honesty! Honesty!

Honesty: Yes.

Journey: Honesty dear, what is that ten thousand you saw?

Honesty speaks in low voice: Love has something to do with it. Journey: Really, I wonder what she have to do with the money.

Okay, you know I got to work at the store, so we will go until Faith gets out of school.

Honesty speaking in low voice crying: I don't want to go after what I did, Mom. I don't trust myself. I just have to stay away from people.

Journey: Oh, Honesty dear, you can't live like that. I just have to keep a close eye on you.

Honesty wrote on paper: "I'm going to go upstairs and draw until you are ready."

Journey: Okay. Let's see what I can eat. (phone rings) Hello. Kavarri: Hi, this is Kavarri. Is Love there?

Journey: No, she's not. Kavarri: Is my daughter there?

Journey: No, she just took off to school. Kavarri: Do you know what school she goes to?

Journey: Umm, I-I don't think I can tell you that. Kavarri: Well, is Love working at the store today? Journey: Yes, she is.

138

Kavarri: I'll just stop by. Thank you for your time. (click) Journey: He got his nerve to ask me all these questions.

(9:00 a.m. in the hospital)

Nurse: Justice, the doctor says that you and your wife can get therapy at home. But I must let you know that your wife's healing is going to be more difficult due to her pregnancy.

Justice: She's not my wife, and I thought so. I mean I knew her healing wasn't going to take place too soon.

Nurse: She's not your wife? So do you have someone to take care of you both until you get well?

Justice: Yes, my ex-wife. She's going to be a big help.

Nurse: Your ex-wife. I could never do that. But I tip my hat off to her. Oh, and the baby is okay. Thank God nothing happened to it.

Justice: Yeah, thank God.

Nurse: Okay, that is all. Get some rest. (Knock at door)

Justice: Come in.

Officer Andrews: Hello, Justice. I'm Officer Andrews, and I come to ask you a few questions. Tell me how did this bad accident happen?

Justice: (coughing) Well, Officer, I was at the red light, and before I knew it I saw a big store truck to my left coming toward me. And he must have lost control because he ran right into me. Oh, my Benz. Glad I had insurance.

Officer Andrews: Wow, and I assume you went flying because when I got there, you were on the other side of the street. And the girl had the car door smashed on her right arm. Well, it's the grace of God you both are alive.

Justice: Yeah, I keep hearing that.

Officer Andrews: Well, take care and get well.

Justice: Thanks. (Back at Love's store)

Kavarri: I'll sit right here and wait until she comes. Oh, and there she is. Yep, court is next week and she is going to drop theses charges. (car door slams) Hello, Love.

Love: Oh, it's you. You scared me. Don't walk up behind me like that. And what are you doing here this early?

Kavarri: Can we talk before you open up? Let's talk inside my car.

Love chuckling: Oh, in your new Mercedes. Wow, I thought I wasn't good enough to sit in this car after our divorce.

Kavarri: Just get in.

Love: Okay. Okay, what do you want! (Door locks)

Love: What are you doing? Open the door.

Kavarri grabs Love by the neck; Listen to me. I want you to call my lawyer and tell him you want to drop the charges and that you are going to tell your lawyer the same. And if you don't, you won't see tomorrow or Faith today to pick her up. Now do it!

Love: I . . . I . . . can't do that.

Kavarri: You know you were wrong for taking Faith and you need to pay for it!

Love: Let go of me! (coughing) Kavarri: Shut up! And dial the number.

Love: What you are doing to me is a crime, and you will do more time when I tell on you.

Kavarri: Love, do it! Dial the number. My hand is going to get tighter, do it!

Love coughing: Okay . . . okay. (dialing) Kavarri: And no games.

Eli: Hello, Eli speaking.

Love: Hi, Eli. Um . . . this is Love. Eli: Hi, you ready for trial next week?

Love in low voice: No, but I'm calling to say I want to drop the charges.

Eli: What? You can't. You and I have a deal. Love: No, forget it!

Eli: The ten thousand I gave you out of the twenty- Five Kavarri gave me. I did that so you can use it until he gets out.

Love: No! That wasn't me. That was someone else. Listen, just drop the charges. (click)

Kavarri: You and that dog of a lawyer played me.

Love sobbing: I hate what you did to me and you make me look like the bad one.

Kavarri: I can't believe you and Eli went against me. Now you two are going to jail. (laughing) Oh yeah, it's your turn, get out of my car. I'll see you in jail. (tires screeching)

Love sobbing: I must call Eli. Eli: Hello, Eli speaking.

Love continued sobbing: Eli, Kavarri had me held hostage and he made me call you, now what?

Eli: You mean he was right there and he heard me? Love: Yes! He did, but now what do we do?

Eli: Let me think because we can get in big trouble for this. I got it. Give me the money back and you press charges against him, and now he got assault and hostage charge to deal with.

Love: No, then he'll be gone even longer and that ten thousand won't even last me. I need month to month for Faith's living.

Eli: Listen, I can get that for you. See, I know your lawyer and I know all the judges. I got pull and he doesn't have proof that you and I did this.

Love: Somehow we got to prove he did this to me without him proving we did what we did. I'm so sorry Eli but I couldn't do a thing.

Eli: Press charges and I will make sure he pays you child support. He can write a check before he goes in. Chat later. Bye.

Journey: (phone ringing) Hello?

Love: Journey, this is Love. Don't come to the store today. I got to go to the police station. I'll tell you later, bye.

Love then puts up CLOSE sign. Journey: Wow, what was that?

Honesty:Screams Mom! Mom!

Journey: Okay, dear. Be there. Yes, dear? Honesty: Look!

Journey: When did you draw this?

Honesty: Just now.

Journey: This is a picture of a hand around Love neck. Oh my God. Honesty: What, Mom?

Journey: Well, Love just called me and said that she had to go the police station. This is getting crazy. (phone rings) Hello?

Kavarri breathing fast: Is Love there? Journey: Who is this?

Kavarri: Me, Kavarri. Is she there! I tried her cell and no answer. Love: No, she is not here.

Kavarri: Don't lie to me! Forget it, I just come over. Bye.

Journey: Oh my God. He hung up on me and he says he is coming over.

(Police station)

Love: Hi, my name is Love Robinson and I would like to speak to Officer Byrd or Andrews.

Officer: Have a seat please.

Officer Byrd: Hello, Love, what can I do for you?

Love: I'm here to press charges against my ex-husband, Kavarri Robinson.

Officer Byrd: Didn't we solve that case?

Love: Yes, and we are going to court for that. But he held me hostage just a few minutes ago, and choked me to try and get me to drop the charges on him.

Officer Andrews: Oh really, okay. We can start the process. I can get most of the information that we have on the kidnap case. But tell me, where did this take place?

Love: It took place outside my business. I hadn't opened up yet and he was parked outside and he came up to me and we talked.

Officer Byrd: Did he seem nervous? Did you notice anything unusual about him?

Love: No, he seemed fine. Then he asked me to get in his car so we can talk, and I did. Then that's when he put his hands around my neck and said I better call his lawyer and tell him I want to drop the charges. Then he said if I didn't do it, that I wouldn't see our daughter. (sobbing) I've never seen him like this.

Officer Byrd: Okay, just relax. I got all the information I need. I think you should keep the store close today or have a friend to go and run it because you've been traumatized. And you should go to the hospital. Wait. Look at your neck.

Love: What, is there a mark?

Officer Byrd: Yes, there is, and let me take a picture. Love: See. He left a mark. I got proof.

Officer Byrd: I need you to go to the hospital and get checked.

Love: No. No, I don't want to go through all that. Can I just go home?

Officer Byrd: Listen this is procedure. Please go. Love: All right, but later.

Officer Byrd: Promise? Love: I promise. Bye.

(Back at Love's home)

Journey: Honesty! Come down here and be careful. Honesty: Yes.

Journey: I think Kavarri is coming by, but I don't know when. But if I'm in the restroom, don't open that door. He has done something very bad and he could be dangerous.

Honesty in low voice: He won't hurt us.

Journey: Just don't, okay. Thanks, dear. Let me call Love's cell. (dialing) (ringing)

Love: Hello?

Journey: Love, are you okay?

Love: Yes, I'm just leaving the police station.

Journey: Well, Kavarri called and said he was coming over. So make sure you look around before you get out of the car.

Love: Oh really. Okay, thanks and I'll be there soon. Journey: Hey, did you not open the store today?

Love: No, and I don't think I will, but I'll see you soon. I think I'm goanna stop by my lawyer's office. You know court is next week and this is why he is going crazy.

Journey: Oh wow, okay, see you soon. (click) (Eli's office)

Kavarri: I would like to see Eli. Receptionist: Umm, he is with a client.

Kavarri: I don't care who he is with. Just tell him I'm here or I'll storm back there.

Receptionist: Okay, okay, calm down. I will go back and tell him. (Kavarri pacing back and forth)

Receptionist: Kavarri, he will see you now. Kavarri: (slam door)

Eli: I see you're here to see me.

Kavarri: I can't believe you, man! I'm hating you right now. How could you use my money to bribe my ex-wife into setting me up? You are in way deep, I can have you put under the jail!

Eli: What are you talking about?

Kavarri: Oh, so now you want to play dumb? I heard everything when Love called you and I should press charges. I'm not going down by myself.

Eli: What were you doing with Love to hear her say that?

Kavarri: Oh no, you are not going to set me up. I came by to tell you, you are fired! And I want my Twenty-Five thousand back.

Eli: Sure. Here it is right here in a check.

Kavarri shocked look: Wha-what you have it? Wait, I want cash!

Eli: Yeah, and if I gave it to her, don't you think I wouldn't be able to give it to you? And I need proof showing I gave you your money back. Now get out of my office.

Kavarri: I'm still pressing charges, and I'll represent myself in court!

I got money!

Eli: You have no proof of what I said to her, and you got your money back.

Kavarri: I'm not going to do time, watch me. Eli: Out of my office!

Kavarri: My pleasure. Receptionist: Sorry, Kavarri.

Kavarri: Yeah, take care. Oh, maybe you can work for me. I pay more. (outside talking to self) Oh boy, what have I done, I-I choked Love. I got to go and tell her I'm sorry.

(Back at the hospital)

Doctor: Morning! Hello, Mr. Robinson. How are you today? Justice: Hey, Doc. I'm okay, what's the verdict?

(Both laugh)

Doctor: Well, you and your girlfriend get to go home tomorrow. Wow, it's been eight weeks already. Hymns' artificial arm is working and so is your leg. You both have some deep cuts that is healing well. The x-rays show on both of you there are some strained muscles in both of your backs that will take time to heal. So you will be getting therapy at home. I'm sure my nurse told you.

Justice: Yeah, which is good. I just want to get back to work.

Doctor: Well, it's going to take a few months, but you'll be back on your feet in no time. Okay, buddy.

Justice: Thanks, Doc. Hey, Doc! Doctor: Yeah?

Justice: Can I and Hymns be in the same room? I'm tired of calling her on the phone ha.

Doctor: Sure. I'll get on that.

Justice: Thanks, Doc. (talking to self) Wow, going home tomorrow, yes.

Nurse: Hi, Justice! They're going to be putting a bed in here for Hymns.

Justice: Nice, even it's for one day.

Nurse: Yeah, even if it's for one day. It shouldn't be long. Lady on intercom: Nurse Angle to room 206

Nurse: Oh, that's me.

Justice: Hey, isn't that Hymns' room?

Angle: Umm, yes. You are right. Let me go see what is going on.

Doctor: It's Hymns. She's having contraction, but we are trying to stop it because she's seven months. I'm sure this is due to the trauma she endured in the accident. Much stress is on the body when a woman is with child.

(Back at Jania's home)

Jania on phone: So he's coming home tomorrow? Oh okay. Is there anything I need to do special for the both of them? No. Okay. No, I'll be fine. It won't be hard for me. If it gets hard I will hire someone to help me. (chuckles) Oh my, what happened? So Hymns won't be coming home with Justice? She may have the baby early. Well, I hope she gets better. Okay, bye. Hmm. So she will be staying and Justice will be here alone with me. I wonder how she is going to take that. Is she reaping what she sowed?

(4:00 p.m., back at Love's home.)

Love: We're home!

Journey: Did you see Kavarri out there anywhere?

Faith: Why would dad be outside? Love: Well, he said he was stopping by.

Faith: Oh, really and you are letting him, Mom?

Love: No! I am not. So what's for dinner? It's it smells good. Journey: I did cook and it is lobster, salad, and bread sticks.

Love: Oh, I'm so glad you cooked that lobster. I've been meaning to cook. I'm going to take a quick shower.

Faith: Me too, school was wild today. I can't wait until I get in the eleventh grade, then I'll only have one more year and I will be out of school.

Journey: Well, don't rush it. Just enjoy high school. Faith: I will. Shower time, then I'll eat.

Journey: Well, it's done.

So I went upstairs to see what Honesty was doing because she left while we all were talking.

Journey walking upstairs: Honesty dear, dinner is ready, what are you doing?

Honesty speaking softly: I'm not feeling good. Something is going on and it has to do with court.

Journey: Is something bad going to happen? Honesty: I-I feel I need to draw something. Journey: Go ahead and draw, let's see.

So she sat down and I walked away to let her do what she needed to do. Five minutes passed by then she called me to look.

Journey: Okay dear, what is this?

Honesty: Phone records.

Journey: Phone records?

Honesty: Yes, wait, Mom. I can't breathe.

Then my daughter fell to the floor. So I ran and got a cold cloth and put it on her head. I didn't want to call Love for help, so I just kept talking to her and re-applying the cold cloth. I looked at what she drew trying to figure out what phone records meant. Then Honesty started mumbling.

Honesty: Love needs t-to get phone records to prove what Kav-rrie did.

Journey: Just take it slow, honey. I think I know what you mean. I think you are saying that Love needs to get phone records to prove something.

Honesty: Ye-yes.

Journey: Somehow I got to get to the bottom of this, Honesty dear. Get up on the bed and lay down and I will bring your food up here.

By this time it was 6:00 p.m. It was getting late so I went downstairs and Faith and Love were already eating.

Love: I was wondering what happened to you. Journey chuckles: Oh, I was talking to Honesty. Love: Is she okay?

Journey: No. It seems like she's coming down with a cold, so I'm going to take her food up to her after I eat.

Faith: Mom, I thought dad was coming by. Maybe I should call him.

Love: No! Not until court is over. Now eat and go to bed. Faith: Sure, Mom, anything you say.

Journey: The lobster is good. Umm, Love, before you go to bed, can I speak with you?

Love: Sure, we can talk now.

Faith: It was good but I'm tired. Night, everyone. (Both say goodnight)

Journey: Tell me, what happened today?

Love: Well, Kavarri tried to make me call his lawyer and tell him I want to drop the charges. So he (crying) choked me to try and make me do it. So I did call his lawyer and told him to drop charges.

Love: But now that I look back, I'm shocked about when Honesty wrote ten thousand on the wall.

Journey: Why are you shocked?

Love: Because Kavarri's lawyer gave me ten thousand after Kavarri paid him to get him off the hook. And he gave it to me to live off of until All this was over. We both thought Kavarri pay for what he did because he thinks his money will keep him out of trouble.

Journey: So basically you and Kavarri's lawyer set him up and you agreed just because you wanted money?

Love: Yes! For Faith. I was hesitating if I should drop charges him go to jail, remember?

Journey: This is too much. Listen, you got to get phone records to prove to the court that you made that call at that time on his cell to his lawyer.

Love: Yeah, I see where you are going with this. His lawyer can get phone records. And there is no way for Kavarri to prove his lawyer said that to me. Yes! Yes! It would be his word against his.

Journey: All I'm saying is there is no way you will be out of money cause you have enough to make it right now.

Love: Yes, I do, but that's my money, I wanted him to use his money to help our child.

Journey: I hear you, but just move on. I think you are safe on your part, hmm. Kavarri never came by.

Love: He knows not to. Journey: Ha, right. Okay, night.

(At 7:00 a.m.)

Journey yarning: It's morning already. Oh boy, what is today going to bring? (shower running)

Love: Morning is here already. Gee, I'm so tired, but it's shower time.

Faith: Time for school already. I'm so tired . . . (turns music on) (Knock at the door)

Journey: Thank God, I'm dressed. Coming! Who can this be?

When I opened the door, it was my ex-husband Jeremiah. I stood in awe.

Journey: Wha-what are you doing here? How did you find us?

Love: Who is it? Kavarri, what are you doing here this time of morning? How could you come over here after what you did to me? Journey, call the police!

Journey: Kavarri? You changed your name! Love: You know him?

Journey: Yes, he's my ex-husband, Honesty's father whom we haven't seen in years.

Love: This is insane! OMG! I think I'm going to vomit. You have another child beside Faith? So our whole marriage was a lie? And Honesty and Faith are sisters?

So Honesty came down stairs and stood in shock. (Back at hospital)

Jania: Hi, I'm here.

Justice: Hi, but can you be a little quiet. Hymns is sleeping over there.

Jania: Oh, she's in here with you now. Well, today you go home. Justice: Yes, and are you ready for this?

Jania whispering: No, I will never be ready. She's waking up. Hymans: Hi, you two.

Jania: Hello, how are you?

Hymns: I'm okay. The baby was trying to come, but they stopped it and I thought I wasn't going to be able to go home. But the doctor said I'm good to go.

Jania: Oh, so you'll be going today too? Justice: Yes, Jania, today.

Jania: Oh that's good. Well, they said I can come get your things. So I'll get your stuff. I got two guys to help me. It seems you brought all your stuff here, was that necessary?

Justice: No. (An hour later)

Jania: We are home and the therapy team is here to help you two get into the house.

Justice: This home looks familiar. Hymns: Oh, Justice, you are funny.

Jania: Justice, don't start. I will go inside to get things ready. Justice: Good idea.

Jania talking to self: Well, they are here and this is surreal. God, get me through this. Oh, you guys, made it in. Well, as you two should know, you are not sleeping in the same room, right?

Justice: Umm, yeah, yeah.

Hymns: We don't have to sleep in the same bed, but we can be in the same room.

Jania: Don't you think that would be kind of strange, put yourself in my shoes.

Justice: Don't start, Jania. It will be fine if we sleep in separate rooms, okay.

Jania: Thank you. So Hymns, here is your room, and Justice . . .

Justice: I know what room I want. I think I know what all the rooms look like when we got this home together.

Jania: Sure, you do. (Back at Love's home) Faith: Dad!

Kavarri: Hey, honey, love you. I think we all need to sit down and talk for the kids' sake.

Faith: Why, what's going on?

Kavarri: Excuse me, my cell is ringing. Hello? Boy, am I glad to hear from you. Yes, I'm ready to join your organization. No, I haven't told anyone; but when I join, are you going to get me off the hook? Like today? Okay, yeah, I know about your meetings, I know you are the leader of the country, yeah I got it. Once I'm in, I'm in. What! You got a shipment, okay. Do you need my plane to do the job? Okay, will talk later. Hey, I need you to take care of that today, before court. Okay, bye.

Journey: Jeremiah! Will you please explain what's going on here? You changed your name, why?

Love: Yes, Kavarri, explain why to us all. Kavarri aka Jeremiah: (Silence)